He passed his trembling hand all about the hole, thinking that his eyes had deceived him.

Then he held the candle in the hole and examined it curiously, trembling more and more. At last he shook so violently that he dropped the candle, and lifted his hands to his head, trying to steady himself, so that he might think. Had he put his gold somewhere else, by a sudden decision last night, and then forgotten it? . . . When there was no other place to be searched, he kneeled down again and felt once more all round the hole. There was no place left to look. The gold was gone. Again he put his trembling hands to his head, and gave a wild ringing scream, the cry of desolation.

A Background Note about *Silas Marner*

Silas Marner is a work of fiction that takes place in England during the early 1800s. The main character is based on a person that George Eliot said she had seen once—an old weaver with a large bag on his back. During her childhood, she would have had quite a few opportunities to see such people. Her father used to take her on errands, sometimes to places where handloom weavers worked.

The reader should keep in mind that there were several varieties of Christianity in England at the time of the novel. The most popular was the Anglican Church, which is the basis for the church in the town of Raveloe, were Silas Marner has come to live. Its members saw church largely as a social function, though an important one. Then there was Methodism, which referred to its churches as chapels. Methodist members were usually much more devout and strict, like the people of Lantern Yard in the community where Silas had lived before.

Silas Marner

GEORGE ELIOT

Edited, and with an Afterword,
by Mary Ann Fugate

 THE TOWNSEND LIBRARY

SILAS MARNER

TP THE TOWNSEND LIBRARY

For more titles in the Townsend Library,
visit our website: **www.townsendpress.com**

All new material in this edition is
copyright © 2005 by Townsend Press.
Printed in the United States of America

0 9 8 7 6 5 4 3 2 1

Townsend Press, Inc.
1038 Industrial Drive
West Berlin, New Jersey 08091

ISBN 1-59194-048-6

Library of Congress Control Number:
2005921077

CONTENTS

AFTERWORD

Chapter 1

In the days when spinning wheels hummed busily in the farmhouses, and even great ladies, dressed in silk and lace, owned toy spinning wheels, there lived a type of man who was pale and small. Compared to the brawny country folk, such men looked like the last of a forgotten race. Dogs barked fiercely whenever one of these alien-looking men appeared on their owner's land, carrying a heavy bag. Indeed, these pale men rarely left home without that mysterious burden. Shepherds usually thought that the bag held nothing but flaxen thread or long rolls of linen. But they were never sure that this trade of weaving, important though it was, could be carried on entirely without the help of the Evil One. In that far-off time superstition surrounded every person or thing that was unwelcome, or even rare, like the visits of the peddler or the knife grinder. No one knew where wandering men came from. How was a man to be explained unless you at least knew somebody who knew his father and mother? To the peasants of old times, the world outside their own direct experience was full of vagueness and mystery. They did not understand the wanderer's life. They even distrusted a settler, if he came from distant parts and was knowledgeable, or skilled in a craft. All cleverness, whether in speech, or in some other art unfamiliar to villagers, was in itself suspicious. Honest folk, raised in an upright manner, were only clever enough to know the signs of the weather. To be quick or good at anything else was attributed to magic, and this is why the scattered linen weavers—emigrants from the town to the country—were always regarded as aliens by their rustic neighbors, and acquired the eccentric habits of the lonely.

In the early part of the century, such a linen weaver, named Silas Marner, worked in a stone cottage that stood among the hedgerows near the village of Raveloe, close to a deserted stone-pit. The strange sound of Silas's loom fascinated the Raveloe boys, who would often stop hunting birds to peep in the window of the stone cottage. They felt both awe and a sense of superiority at the mysterious action of the loom and the weaver. But sometimes Marner, pausing to correct his thread, became aware of the small scoundrels. Though he hated to take the time, their intrusion annoyed him so much that he would leave his loom, and, opening the door, would give them a look that always made them take to their legs in terror. Those large brown bulging eyes in Silas Marner's pale face seemed made less for seeing than for cursing a boy with cramp, rickets, or a deformed mouth. Perhaps they had heard their fathers and mothers hint that Silas Marner could cure folks' rheumatism if he had a mind, and that if you praised the devil, he might save you the cost of the doctor. Such examples of the old demon-worship could be heard among the elder peasants, for uneducated people do not associate power with a good heart. Neither could they imagine a higher being who was full of goodness, for they had no religion, and their lives of hard labor taught them that pain was more frequent than pleasure.

Many of the old ways lingered in Raveloe, unchanged by new ones. Yet it wasn't one of those forgotten places on the outskirts of civilization, inhabited only by sheep and shepherds. On the contrary, it lay in the rich central plain of Merry England, and held highly profitable farms. But it was nestled in a snug well-wooded hollow, an hour's journey on horseback from any turnpike, and off the beaten path. It was an important-looking village, with a fine old church and large churchyard in the heart of it, and two or three large brick-and-stone homes standing close to the road. However, the village showed at once the limits of its social life, and told the experienced observer that Raveloe had no great park and manor-house, but only several people who farmed quite badly and still made enough to have a jolly Christmas and Easter.

It was fifteen years since Silas Marner had come to Raveloe. Back then he was simply a pallid young man, with prominent nearsighted brown eyes, whose appearance would not have surprised people of average culture and experience. But his new neighbors thought his looks were as mysterious as his occupation. So, too, his homeland called "North'ard" and his way of life: he never invited visitors, or strolled into the village to drink a pint at the Rainbow or gossip at the wheelwright's. He sought no man or woman, except for matters of his business, and it was soon clear to the Raveloe lasses that they were as safe from his attentions as from those of a dead man. This comparison stemmed from more than just his pale face and strange eyes.

Jem Rodney, the mole-catcher, swore that

one evening as he was returning home, he saw Silas Marner leaning against a ledge with a heavy bag on his back, instead of resting the bag on the ledge as a sane person would have done. On approaching him, he saw that Marner's eyes were set like a dead man's. Jem spoke to him and shook him, and his limbs were stiff, his hands clutching the bag as if they'd been made of iron. But just as he had decided that the weaver was dead, he returned to normal in the blink of an eye, said "Goodnight," and walked off. All this Jem swore he had seen, saying also that it was the very day he had been mole-catching on Squire Cass's land, down by the old saw pit.

Some said Marner must have been in a "fit," a word used to explain things that were not understood. But the argumentative Mr. Macey, clerk of the parish, shook his head, and asked if anybody could have a fit and not fall down. Since a fit was a stroke, it should partly take away the use of a man's limbs. No stroke would let a man stand on his legs, and later walk off. But a man's soul might be loose from his body, going out and in, like a bird out of its nest and back. That was how folks got too wise, for they went to school in this exposed state, learning more than they could normally.

And where did Master Marner get his knowledge of herbs from, and spells too? Jem

Rodney's story was not surprising, considering how Marner had cured Sally Oates, and made her sleep like a baby, when her heart had been beating enough to burst her body, for more than two months under the doctor's care. He could cure more folks if he wanted to, but people thought you shouldn't speak badly of him, if only to keep him from doing you harm.

It was partly because of this vague fear that Marner was not persecuted as he otherwise would have been. But the fact that the old linen weaver in the neighboring parish was dead also made Marner valuable to the richer housewives of the district. Even for the wealthier cottagers, who had a bit of yarn at the year's end, his usefulness balanced out their suspicions of him. The years had rolled on without changing anyone's impression of Marner, except that he became less and less of a novelty. At the end of fifteen years the Raveloe men said just the same things about Silas Marner as at the beginning. They did not say them quite so often, but they believed them much more strongly when they did say them. There was only one important addition, which was that Master Marner had saved up a lot of money somewhere, and that he could buy up "bigger men" than himself.

But while opinion concerning him had remained nearly the same, and his daily habits had not seemed to change, Marner's inner life had been complex, as that of a passionate person must be when he has been condemned to solitude. His life, before he came to Raveloe, had been filled with the social connections that are part of the life of an artisan belonging to a small religious group, where the poorest man can distinguish himself by speaking well and participating in the decisions of his community. Marner was highly regarded in that little hidden world, known to itself as the church assembling in Lantern Yard. He was believed to be a young man of exemplary life and intense faith. People had developed a peculiar interest in him ever since he had fallen, at a prayer meeting, into a mysterious and rigid state, which, lasting for an hour or more, had been mistaken for death. To look for a medical explanation would have been seen as a spiritual mistake.

Silas was evidently a brother selected for a certain service, though he experienced no spiritual vision during his trance. A less truthful man might have been tempted to make up a vision, and a less sane man might have believed in such a creation. But Silas was both sane and honest, though, as with many honest and passionate men, culture had not given him a way to cultivate his sense of mystery, and so he tried to acquire knowledge. He had inherited from his mother some experience with preparing and using medicinal herbs, but in recent years he doubted whether it was right to apply this knowledge, believing that herbs could not work without prayer, and that prayer might be enough by itself. So the old delight in wandering in the fields in search of foxglove, dandelion, and coltsfoot, began to seem like a temptation.

Among the members of his church there was one young man, a little older than himself, who was his close friend. This friend, named William Dane, was also regarded as a shining example of youthful piety, though somewhat given to bullying and arrogance. But whatever blemishes others might see in William, to his friend's mind he was faultless.

Marner had one of those gullible self-doubting natures that admire other people's confidence. The look of trust and simplicity in Marner's face strongly contrasted the smugness and pride that lurked in the narrow slanting eyes and compressed lips of William Dane. The two friends often talked about the assurance of salvation. Silas confessed that he felt nothing more secure than hope mingled with fear, and listened with wonder when William boasted of being confident ever since he had dreamed that he saw the words "calling and election sure" standing by themselves on a white page in the open Bible.

Silas thought that nothing could hurt their friendship, not even his other attachment of a closer kind. For some months he had been engaged to a young servant-woman, waiting only to save up a little more money before getting married. He was delighted that Sarah did not object to William's occasional presence at their Sunday appointments. It was around this time that Silas's fit occurred during the prayer meeting. Afterward, everyone supported Silas with sympathy and interest, except for William, who suggested that his trance looked more like a visitation of Satan than proof of God's favor. He urged Silas not to hide the evil in his soul. Silas, thinking William was only doing his duty as a friend, felt no resentment, but only pain that William doubted him.

But his anxiety grew as Sarah seemed to shrink from him. He asked her if she wished to break off their engagement, but she denied this. Their engagement was known to the church, and had been recognized in the prayer meetings. It could not be broken off without strict investigation, and Sarah did not have a good reason for doing so.

At this time the senior deacon became dangerously ill, and, being a childless widower, he was tended night and day by some of the younger church members. Silas frequently took

his turn in the vigil with William, the one reliev-
ing the other at two in the morning. The old
man unexpectedly seemed on the way to recov-
ery, when one night Silas, sitting up by his bed-
side, saw that he had stopped breathing. The
candle was burning low, and he lifted it to see
the patient's face distinctly. Examination convinced him that the deacon was dead—had been
dead some time, for the limbs were rigid. Silas
asked himself if he had been asleep, and looked
at the clock: it was already four in the morning.
How was it that William had not come?

Anxious, he went for help, and soon several
friends assembled in the house, the minister
among them. Silas left for work, wishing he had
found out why William hadn't shown. At six
o'clock, as he was thinking of going to find him,
William came, and with him the minister. They
summoned him to Lantern Yard, to meet the
church members. When Silas asked why, the only
reply was, "You will hear." Nothing further was
said until Silas was seated in the vestry, in front
of the minister, with the eyes of the congregation
solemnly upon him. Then the minister, taking
out a pocketknife, showed it to Silas, and asked
him if he knew where he had left that knife. Silas,
trembling at this strange interrogation, said he
did not know that he had left it anywhere out of
his own pocket. He was then told not to hide his

sin, but to confess and repent.

The knife had been found in the departed deacon's dresser, where the little bag of church money usually lay, which the minister himself had seen the day before. Some hand had removed that bag, and whose hand could it be, if not that of the man to whom the knife belonged? For some time Silas was silent with astonishment. Then he said, "God will clear me: I know nothing about the knife being there, or the money being gone. Search me and my house. You will find nothing but three pounds and five shillings of my own savings, which William Dane knows I have had these six months." At this William groaned, and the minister said, "The proof is heavy against you, brother Marner. The money was taken last night, and only you were with our departed brother, for William Dane fell ill suddenly. You yourself said that he did not come, and, moreover, you neglected the dead body."

"I must have slept," said Silas. Then, after a pause, he added, "Or I must have had another visitation like before, so that the thief came and went while I was out of my body. But, I say again, search me and my house, for I have been nowhere else."

The search was made, and William Dane found the well-known bag, empty, tucked behind the chest of drawers in Silas's chamber! Then William urged his friend to confess, and not to hide his sin any longer. Silas looked reproachfully at him, and said, "William, for nine years you have known me, have I ever told a lie? Indeed, God will clear me."

"Brother," said William, "how do I know what you may have done in the secret chambers of your heart, to fall under Satan's power?"

Silas's face flushed, and he seemed about to speak, when some inward shock touched him. His flush drained away, and, trembling, he spoke to William.

"I remember now—the knife wasn't in my pocket."

William said, "I know nothing of what you mean." The other people asked Silas where the knife had been, but he would not tell. He only said, "I am deeply wounded, and I can say nothing. God will clear me."

The members returned to the vestry to deliberate further. The principles of the church forbid using legal methods to deal with the problem. But the members had to find out the truth, and they decided to pray and draw lots. Silas knelt with his brethren, hoping that God would prove him innocent, and feeling that he had lost trust in his fellow man. The lots declared that Silas Marner was guilty. He was solemnly suspended from church membership, and ordered to return the stolen money. Only after confessing could he be received once more within the folds of the church.

Marner listened in silence. At last, when everyone rose to depart, he went to William Dane and said, in a shaking voice, "The last time I remember using my knife, was when I took it out to cut a strap for you. I don't remember putting it in my pocket again. You stole the money, and you have woven a plot to lay the sin at my door. But you are likely to get away with it. There is no just God, who governs the earth righteously, but a God of lies, who persecutes the innocent."

The members shuddered at this blasphemy. William said meekly, "I leave our brethren to judge whether this is the voice of Satan. I can do nothing but pray for you, Silas."

Poor Marner went out with despair in his soul, his trust in God and man deeply shaken almost to the point of madness. In his bitterness, he said to himself, "Sarah will reject me too." And he reflected that, if she did not believe the testimony against him, her whole faith must be as destroyed as his was.

Marner went home, and for a whole day sat alone, stunned by despair, without any desire to go to Sarah and attempt to convince her of his innocence. The second day he escaped his thoughts by getting into his loom and working away as usual. After a few hours, the minister and one of the deacons delivered a message from Sarah, that she had ended their engagement. Silas received the message in silence, and then turned away from the messengers to work at his loom again. A little more than a month later, Sarah married William Dane, and not long afterward Silas Marner left town.

Chapter 2

Even educated people sometimes find it hard to hold onto their faith and sense of identity when they are suddenly transported to a new land, where people know nothing of their history, and share none of their ideas, where even the scenery is strange, and people look different. In this type of exile, the past becomes dreamy because its symbols have all vanished, and the present too is dreamy because it is linked with no memories. But even these people cannot imagine the effect on a simple weaver like Silas Marner, when he left his own country and people and came to settle in Raveloe.

Nothing could be more unlike his native town than this low, wooded region, where he felt hidden from the heavens by the tall trees and hedgerows. When he rose in the deep morning quiet and looked out at the dewy brambles and tufted grass, none of it resembled the life in Lantern Yard, which had once been the most important place on earth to him. The whitewashed walls, the little pews where familiar figures spoke in familiar voices, the pulpit where the minister delivered sermons and swayed to and fro, the singing of the hymns—these things had been the work of God to Marner. They embodied Christianity and God's kingdom upon earth.

And what could be more unlike that Lantern Yard world than the world in Raveloe? Raveloe had its orchards filled with neglected fruit, the large church in the wide churchyard, where few attended services, purple-faced farmers jogging along the lanes or turning in at the Rainbow, homesteads where men ate heartily and slept in the light of the evening hearth, and women stored up enough linen for the next lifetime.

In the early ages of the world, it was believed that each territory was inhabited and ruled by its own gods, so that a man could cross a border and be out of the reach of his native deities. Poor Silas felt like one of those primitive men who had fled his maker. It seemed to him that the Power he had trusted at the prayer meetings was very far away from this land. Here, men knew nothing of that trust, which, for him, had turned to bitterness.

His first action after the shock had been to work in his loom. Now that he was in Raveloe, he worked far into the night to finish Mrs. Osgood's table linen sooner than she expected, without thinking of the money he would earn. He seemed to weave like the spider, from pure impulse, without reflection. Every man's work, pursued steadily in this way, tends to become an end in itself, and so bridges the loveless gaps of his life. Then there were the calls of hunger, and Silas, in his solitude, had to provide his own breakfast, lunch, and supper, to fetch his own water from the well, and put his own kettle on the fire. All these activities helped, along with the weaving, to reduce his life to the unquestioning activity of a spinning insect. He hated the thought of the past, he felt no love for his neighbors, and the future was dark, for there was no Unseen Love that cared for him.

At last Mrs. Osgood's table linen was finished, and Silas was paid in gold. His earnings in his native town had been much lower, and a large proportion had gone to charity. Now, for the first time in his life, he had five bright guineas put into his hand. No one expected a share, and he loved no one enough to offer. But what were guineas to him who had no future? Still, it was pleasant to feel them in his palm, and look at their bright faces. For twenty years, money had been for him a symbol of earthly good, and the immediate result of toil. He had loved it little in the years when every penny had its purpose for him, for he loved the purpose then. But now, when all purpose was gone, the coins themselves triggered the beginning of desire. As Silas walked homeward across the fields in the twilight, he drew out the money and thought it was brighter in the gathering gloom.

About this time something happened that opened the possibility of fellowship with his neighbors. One day, taking a pair of shoes to be mended, he saw the cobbler's wife seated by the fire, suffering from the terrible symptoms of heart disease, which had killed his mother. He felt a rush of pity, and, remembering the relief his mother had found in a simple medicine of foxglove, he promised Sally Oates to bring her something that would help, since the doctor did her no good.

In this act of charity, Silas felt, for the first time since he had come to Raveloe, a sense of unity between his past and present life, which might have been the beginning of his rescue from his insectlike existence. But Sally Oates's disease had made her very important among the neighbors, and the fact of her having found relief from drinking Silas Marner's "stuff" became a matter of general discussion. When Doctor Kimble gave someone medicine, it was natural that it should have an effect. But when a weaver, who came from nobody knew where, worked wonders with a bottle of brown water, it was obviously magic.

Such a thing had not happened since the Wise Woman at Tarley died, who had charms as well as "stuff." Everybody went to her when their children had fits. Silas Marner must be a person of the same sort, for how did he know what would improve Sally Oates's breathing? The Wise Woman had words that she muttered to herself, so that you couldn't hear what they were. There were women in Raveloe, at that present time, who had worn one of the Wise Woman's little bags round their necks, and, as a result, had never had an idiot child, as Ann Coulter had. Silas Marner could very likely do as much, and more. Now it made sense that he had come from unknown parts and was so funny looking. But Sally Oates must not tell the doctor, for he would turn against Marner. He was always angry about the Wise Woman, and used to threaten those who went to her that he would not help them anymore.

Silas now found himself suddenly beset by mothers who wanted him to charm away the whooping cough, or bring back their breast milk, and by men who wanted treatment for rheumatism or arthritis. To plead their causes, the applicants brought silver, and Silas might have made a profit from charms as well as from drugs. But he was never tempted, being an honest man. With growing irritation, he sent one after another away. Eventually, hope in his wisdom changed into dread, for no one believed him when he said he knew no charms and could work no cures. Every man and woman who had an accident or a new attack after applying to him blamed Master Marner's ill will and irritated glances. Thus it happened that his charity toward Sally Oates, which had given him a fleeting sense of community, worsened the relations between him and his neighbors, and made his isolation more complete.

Gradually the guineas, the crowns, and the half-crowns grew to a heap, and Marner spent less and less, trying to keep his output high and expenses low. In the same way that people make repetitive movements out of boredom, which turn into habit, Marner grew into the habit of hoarding money. Every added guinea, while it was itself a satisfaction, bred a new desire. The money had come to mark off his weaving into periods, and the money not only grew, but it remained with him. He began to think it was conscious of him, as his loom was. He would never have exchanged those coins, which had become familiar, for other coins with unknown faces. He handled and counted them until their form and color were like water for his thirst. But it was only at night, when his work was done, that he drew them out to enjoy their companionship. He had taken up some bricks in his floor underneath his loom, and here he had made a hole in which he set the iron pot containing his guineas and silver coins. He covered the bricks with sand whenever he replaced them, though a robbery did not seem likely. Lots of old laborers hoarded their savings, probably inside their houses. And their rustic neighbors, though not all of them as honest as their ancestors, were not daring enough to steal. How could they have spent the money in their own village without betraying themselves? They would be obliged to "run away"—an idea as dark and dubious as a balloon journey.

So, year after year, Silas Marner had lived in this solitude, his guineas rising in the iron pot, and his life narrowing into a single vein of desire and satisfaction unrelated to any other being. His life had reduced itself to the functions of weaving and hoarding, without any higher purpose. Marner's face and body became mere mechanical tools for operating the objects of his life, so that he seemed nothing more than a handle or a crooked tube, which has no function by itself. The prominent eyes, which used to look trusting and dreamy, now looked as if they had been made to see only one kind of thing that was very small, like tiny grain. He was so withered and yellow, that, though he was not yet forty, the children always called him "Old Master Marner."

Yet even in this stage of withering a little incident happened that showed that not all his affection was gone. Every day, he fetched his water from a well a couple of fields off, using a brown earthenware pot, which he held as his most precious utensil among his few possessions. It had been his companion for twelve years, always standing on the same spot, always lending its handle to him in the early morning. One day as he was returning from the well, he stumbled, and his brown pot, falling with force against the stones, broke in three pieces. Silas picked up the pieces and carried them home with grief in his heart. The brown pot could never be of use to him anymore, but he stuck the bits together and propped the ruin in its old place for a memorial.

Thus went Silas Marner's life until the fifteenth year after he came to Raveloe. The livelong day he sat in his loom, his ear filled with its monotony, his eyes close on the linen, his muscles moving with even repetition. But at night he closed his shutters, locked his doors, and brought out his gold. Long ago the heap of coins had become too large for the iron pot, and he had made two thick leather bags, which fit nicely in their hiding place. How the guineas shone as they came pouring out of the dark leather mouths! There was not as much silver as gold, because his long pieces of linen were mostly paid for in gold, and he bought his provisions with silver. He loved the guineas best, but he would not change the silver, the crowns and half-crowns that were products of his labor. He loved them all. He spread them out in heaps and bathed his hands in them. Then he counted them and set them up in regular piles, and felt their rounded outline between his thumb and fingers, thinking fondly of the guineas that would be earned by the work currently in his loom, as if they had been unborn children. He thought of the guineas that would arrive in the coming years, which spread far away before him, the end quite hidden by countless days of weaving. No wonder his thoughts were still with his loom and his money when he made his journeys through the fields and lanes to fetch and carry home his work, so that he never wandered off in search of the once familiar herbs. They, too, belonged to the past, from which his life had shrunk away, like a stream that strays from the river to cut a groove for itself in the barren sand.

But around Christmas of that fifteenth year, a second great change came to Marner's life, and his history combined in a most unusual way with the life of his neighbors.

Chapter 3

The greatest man in Raveloe was Squire Cass, who lived in the large red house with the stables behind it, nearly opposite the church. He was only one among several wealthy landowners, but he alone had the title of Squire. Mr. Osgood's family had been in town a very long time, but he merely owned the farm he occupied, while Squire Cass had a tenant or two.

Because there was still a war on, the wealthy people were able to enjoy their extravagant habits, which would be impossible when the prices finally fell. The rich of Raveloe ate and drank freely, accepting gout and apoplexy as things that ran mysteriously in respectable families. The poor people thought that the rich were entitled to lead a jolly life. Besides, the scraps from their feasts were passed eventually to the poor. The Raveloe feasts were like the rounds of beef and the barrels of ale—they were on a large scale, and lasted a good while, especially in the winter. Ladies packed up their best gowns and wigs in bandboxes, and forded streams in the rain and snow to reach their neighbors' houses, which they enjoyed in succession for the whole season. As soon as Squire Cass's meals grew a bit tiresome, his guests had only to walk a little higher up the village to Mr. Osgood's, at the Orchards, and they found hams, pork pies with the scent of the fire in them, spun butter in all its freshness—everything, in fact, that appetites at leisure could desire.

The Squire's wife had died long ago, and the Red House lacked that presence of the wife and mother that is the fountain of wholesome love and fear in parlor and kitchen. This explained not only the triumph of quantity over quality in the holiday provisions, but also the Squire's habit of frequenting the Rainbow. Perhaps it was also the reason that his sons had turned out rather badly.

Raveloe was not a morally strict place, but it was said that the Squire should not keep all his sons at home in idleness. Though people thought that young men should have some freedom if their fathers could afford it, they shook their heads over the behavior of the Squire's second son, Dunstan, commonly called Dunsey Cass. He was a spiteful fellow, who loved to drink and gamble. As long as he did not disgrace his father, however, his behavior did not matter as much as that of Mr. Godfrey, the oldest. Godfrey was a fine, good-natured young man who was to inherit the land some day, but he had been acting like his brother lately. If he went on in that way, he would lose Miss Nancy Lammeter. It was well-known that she had doubted him ever since last Pentecost, when there was so much talk about the two brothers being away for days and days.

There was something wrong, for Mr. Godfrey didn't look half so fresh and open as he used to. At one time everybody was saying what a handsome couple he and Miss Nancy Lammeter would make. If she became mistress at the Red House, there would be a fine change, for the Lammeters had been brought up to be efficient and maintain high standards. Such a daughter-in-law would save the old Squire some money, even if she never brought a penny with her dowry. It was said that his financial situation was not entirely secure. But if Mr. Godfrey didn't turn over a new leaf, he might have to say goodbye to Miss Nancy Lammeter.

It was the once hopeful Godfrey who was standing, with his hands in his side pockets and his back to the fire, in the dark parlor, one late November afternoon in that fifteenth year of Silas Marner's life at Raveloe. The fading gray light fell dimly on the walls decorated with guns, whips, and foxes' brushes, on coats and hats flung on the chairs, on tankards sending forth a scent of flat ale, and on a half-choked fire, with tobacco pipes propped up in the chimney corners. It was a gloomy scene, matched by the expression on Godfrey's pale face. He seemed to be waiting and listening for someone's approach, and soon the sound of a heavy step, with an accompanying whistle, was heard across the large empty entrance hall.

The door opened, and a heavy young man entered, with the cheery, flushed face that marks the first stage of intoxication. It was Dunsey, and at the sight of him Godfrey's face changed from gloomy to hateful. The handsome brown spaniel that lay on the hearth retreated under a chair.

"Well, Master Godfrey, what do you want with me?" said Dunsey, in a mocking tone. "Since you're my elder, I was obliged to come when you sent for me."

"Just shake yourself sober and listen, will you?" said Godfrey, savagely. He had himself been drinking more than was good for him, trying to turn his gloom into uncalculating anger.

"I must hand over that rent of Fowler's to the Squire, or else tell him I gave it to you. He's threatening to evict him, and it'll all be out soon, whether I tell him or not. He said, just now, before he went out, he should send word to Cox to evict him, if Fowler didn't come and pay up his account this week. The Squire's short of cash and won't take any nonsense. You know what he threatened, if he ever found you making away with his money again. So, get the money, and pretty quickly, will you?"

"Oh!" said Dunsey, sneering, coming nearer to his brother and looking in his face. "Suppose, now, you get the money yourself, and save me the trouble, eh? Since you were so kind as to hand it over to me, you'll not refuse me the kindness to pay it back for me. It was your brotherly love that made you do it, you know."

Godfrey bit his lips and clenched his fist. "Don't come near me with that look, else I'll knock you down."

"Oh no, you won't," said Dunsey, turning away on his heel, however. "Because I'm such a good-natured brother, you know. I could get you turned out of house and home, and cut off with a shilling any day. I could tell the Squire how his handsome son was married to that nice young woman, Molly Farren, and was very unhappy because he couldn't live with his drunken wife, and I should slip into your place as comfortable as could be. But you see, I won't do it—I'm so easy and good-natured. You'll take any trouble for me. You'll get the hundred pounds for me—I know you will."

"How can I get the money?" said Godfrey, quivering. "I haven't a shilling to bless myself with. And it's a lie that you'd slip into my place. You'd get yourself turned out too, that's all. For if you begin telling tales, I'll follow. Bob's my father's favorite—you know that very well. He'd only think himself well rid of you."

"Never mind," said Dunsey, nodding his head sideways as he looked out of the window. "I would love to leave with you—you're such a handsome brother, and we've always been so fond of quarreling with one another. I shouldn't know what to do without you. But I know you prefer for us both to stay at home together. So you'll manage to get that little sum o' money, and I'll bid you goodbye, though I'm sorry to part."

Dunstan was moving off, but Godfrey rushed after him and seized him by the arm, saying, with an oath, "I tell you, I have no money, and I can't get any."

"Borrow from old Kimble."

"I tell you, he won't lend me any more, and I shan't ask him."

"Well, then, sell Wildfire."

"But I must have the money soon."

"Well, you've only got to ride him to the hunt tomorrow. There'll be Bryce and Keating there, for sure. You'll get plenty of offers."

"And I'll get back home at eight o'clock, splashed up to the chin. I'm going to Mrs. Osgood's birthday dance."

"Oho!" said Dunsey, turning his head on one side, and speaking in a prim voice. "And there's sweet Miss Nancy coming. We shall dance with her, and promise never to be naughty again, and —"

"Hold your tongue about Miss Nancy, you fool," said Godfrey, turning red, "else I'll throttle you."

"What for?" said Dunsey, still in an artificial tone, but taking a whip from the table and beating the butt end of it on his palm. "You've a very good chance. Molly might take a drop too much laudanum some day, and make a widower of you. Miss Nancy wouldn't mind being a second wife, if she didn't know it. And you've got a good-natured brother, who'll keep your secret well, because you'll be so very obliging to him."

Godfrey, quivering, said, "My patience is pretty near at an end. If you'd a little more sharpness in you, you might know that you may push a man a bit too far, and make one leap as easy as another. I may as well tell the Squire everything myself—it would get you off my back, if I got nothing else. And, after all, he'll know sooner or later. She's been threatening to come here herself and tell him. So, don't flatter yourself that your secrecy's worth any price you choose to ask. If you drain me of money till I have nothing to pacify her with, then she'll do as she threatens someday. So, I'll tell my father everything myself, and you may go to the devil."

Dunsey perceived that he had overshot his mark, and that there was a point at which even the hesitating Godfrey might be driven into decision. But he said, with an air of unconcern, "As you please; but I'll have a glass of ale first." And ringing the bell, he threw himself across two chairs, and began to rap the window seat with the handle of his whip.

Godfrey stood, still with his back to the fire, uneasily moving his fingers among the contents of his side pockets, and looking at the floor. That big muscular frame of his held plenty of animal courage, but it did not help him when the danger could neither be knocked down nor throttled. No sooner had he threatened to defy Dunstan than the miserable consequences of such a step seemed worse than the present evil. The results of confession were certain, whereas betrayal was not certain.

The disinherited son of a small squire, unwilling to work or beg, was almost as helpless as an uprooted tree. Perhaps working would have been possible if Nancy Lammeter could be won on those terms. But, since he was sure to lose her as well as the inheritance, and must break every tie but the one that degraded him, he could imagine no future for himself except the army. That was the most desperate step, short of suicide, in the eyes of respectable families. No! He would rather trust chance than choice. He would rather go on sitting at the feast, and sipping the wine he loved, with the sword hanging over him and terror in his heart, than rush away into the cold darkness where there was no pleasure left. Selling his horse began to seem easy, compared with carrying out his own threat. But his pride would not let him restart the conversation without continuing the quarrel. Dunstan was waiting for this, and took his ale in smaller drinks than usual.

"It's just like you," Godfrey burst out, in a bitter tone, "to talk about my selling Wildfire in that cool way—the last thing I've got to call my own, and the best bit of horseflesh I ever had in my life. And if you'd got a spark of pride in you, you'd be ashamed to see the stables emptied, and everybody sneering about it. But it's my belief you'd sell yourself, if it was only for the pleasure of making somebody feel he'd got a bad bargain."

"Aye, aye," said Dunstan, very calmly, "you're right about that. You know I love to strike a bargain, for which reason I advise you to let me sell Wildfire. I'd ride him to the hunt tomorrow for you, with pleasure. I won't look so handsome as you in the saddle, but it's the horse they'll bid for, and not the rider."

"Yes, I daresay—trust my horse to you!"

"As you please," said Dunstan, rapping the window seat again with an air of great unconcern. "It's you that has to pay Fowler's money. It's none of my business. You received the money from him when you went to Bramcote, and you told the Squire it wasn't paid. I'd nothing to do with that. You chose to give it to me. If you don't want to pay the money, then don't. I don't care. But I was willing to help you by selling the horse, since it's not convenient for you to go so far tomorrow."

Godfrey was silent for some moments. He would have liked to spring on Dunstan, wrench the whip from his hand, and flog him to within an inch of his life. It was not physical fear that stopped him, but another sort of fear, which was fed by feelings stronger even than his resentment. When he spoke again, it was in a half-agreeable tone.

"Well, you're serious about the horse, eh? You'll sell him fair, and hand over the money? If you don't, you know, everything is ruined, for I've got nothing else. And you'll have less pleasure in pulling the house over my head, when your own skull's to be broken too."

"Aye, aye," said Dunstan, rising. "All right. I thought you'd come round. I'll get you a hundred and twenty for him, if I get you a penny."

"But it'll perhaps rain cats and dogs tomorrow, as it did yesterday, and then you can't go," said Godfrey, hardly knowing whether he wished for that obstacle or not.

"Not a chance," said Dunstan. "I'm always lucky in my weather. It might rain if you wanted to go yourself. You've got the beauty, you see, and I've got the luck, so you must keep me by you. You'll never get along without me."

"Confound you, hold your tongue!" said Godfrey, impetuously. "And take care to keep sober tomorrow, else you'll get thrown on your head coming home, and Wildfire might be the worse for it."

"Make your tender heart easy," said Dunstan, opening the door. "I never get drunk when I've got a bargain to make. It would spoil the fun. Besides, whenever I fall, I'm bound to fall on my legs."

With that, Dunstan slammed the door

behind him, and left Godfrey to think bitterly about his personal circumstances, now unbroken from day to day except by the excitement of sporting, drinking, card-playing, or the rarer pleasure of seeing Miss Nancy Lammeter. That was the condition of Godfrey Cass in this twenty-sixth year of his life. As for his secret marriage, it was an ugly story of low passion, delusion, and waking from delusion, which should not be dragged from the privacy of Godfrey's bitter memory. He had long known that the delusion was part of a trap laid for him by Dunstan, whose hatred was fulfilled by his brother's degrading marriage. If Godfrey could have felt himself simply a victim, he could have borne his fate better. And if the curses he muttered half aloud when he was alone had had no other object than Dunstan's diabolical cunning, he might have owned up to the consequences. But he had something else to curse—his own vicious folly, which now seemed as mad and unaccountable to him as almost all our follies and vices do when their reasons have long passed away.

For four years he had thought of Nancy Lammeter, and wooed her with patient worship, as the woman who made him think of the future with joy. She would be his wife, and would make home lovely to him, as his father's home had never been. It would be easy, when she was always near, to shake off those foolish habits that were not pleasures, but only feverish ways of avoiding loneliness. Godfrey had an essentially domestic nature, brought up in a cheerless home, without any household order. His need of some tender permanent affection, the longing for some better influence, caused the neatness and purity of the Lammeter household to seem like those fresh bright hours of the morning when temptations go to sleep and the voice of the good angel arrives, inviting industry, sobriety, and peace. And yet the hope of this paradise had not been enough to save him from behavior that shut him out of it forever. Instead of holding onto the strong silken rope by which Nancy would have drawn him up to the safe green banks, he had let himself be dragged back into mud and slime, in which it was useless to struggle.

Still, there was one position worse than the present: it was the position he would be in when the ugly secret was disclosed. More than anything, he wanted to avoid the evil day when his father would punish him for hurting the family pride. He would lose the dignity of his family's name, which, after all, was a sort of reason for living. And he would lose forever the company of Nancy Lammeter. The longer he waited, the less harsh the consequences might be, and the more opportunities of seeing Nancy, and determining her feelings for him. Every few weeks, he yearned to see her, and one of those fits of yearning was on him now. This would have been reason enough to trust Wildfire to Dunstan. But it also happened that the morning's meet was near Batherley, the town where the unhappy woman lived, who became more disgusting to him every day. The chains that a man creates for himself by doing wrong will breed hate in the kindest nature. The good-humored, affection-ate Godfrey Cass was fast becoming a bitter man, visited by cruel wishes.

What was he to do this evening to pass the time? He might as well go to the Rainbow, and hear the talk about the cock-fighting. Every-body was there, and what else was there to be done? Though, for his own part, he did not care a button for cock-fighting. Snuff, the brown spaniel, who had placed herself in front of him, and had been watching him for some time, now jumped up in impatience for the expected caress. But Godfrey thrust her away without looking at her, and left the room, followed humbly by the forgiving Snuff—perhaps because she saw no other choice.

Chapter 4

Dunstan Cass, setting off in the raw morning, had to take the lane that passed by the piece of unenclosed ground called the Stone Pit, where stood the cottage that belonged for fifteen years to Silas Marner. The spot looked very dreary at this season, with the moist trodden clay about it, and the red, muddy water high up in the deserted quarry. That was Dunstan's first thought as he approached it. The second was that the old fool of a weaver, whose loom he heard rattling already, had a great deal of money hidden somewhere. How was it that he, Dunstan Cass, who had often heard talk of Marner's miserliness, had never thought of suggesting to Godfrey that he should frighten or persuade the old fellow into lending the money on the excellent security of the young Squire's future? The idea seemed obvious, especially since Marner's stash was likely to be large enough to allow Godfrey to accommodate his faithful brother. He almost turned the horse's head toward home again, since Godfrey would snatch eagerly at a plan that might save him from parting with Wildfire. But at that moment, Dunstan decided to go on to the hunt, for he preferred that Master Godfrey should be displeased. Moreover, Dunstan enjoyed the important position of having a horse to sell, and the opportunity of driving a bargain, swaggering, and possibly taking somebody in. He would have the satisfaction of selling his brother's horse, and the further satisfaction of arranging that Godfrey borrow Marner's money. So he rode on.

Bryce and Keating were there, as Dunstan was quite sure they would be—he was such a lucky fellow.

"Heyday!" said Bryce, who had long had his eye on Wildfire, "you're on your brother's horse today. Why's that?"

"Oh, I've traded with him," said Dunstan, whose delight in lying was not to be lessened by the likelihood that his hearer would not believe him. "Wildfire's mine now."

"What! Has he traded with you for that big-boned nag of yours?" said Bryce, quite aware that he should get another lie in reply.

"Oh, there was a little account between us," said Dunsey, carelessly, "and Wildfire made it even. I accommodated him by taking the horse, though it was against my will, for I'd got an itch for a mare of Jortin's—as rare a bit o' blood as ever you threw your leg across. But I shall keep Wildfire, now I've got him, though I'd a bid of a hundred and fifty for him the other day, from a man over at Flitton. He's buying for Lord Cromleck—a fellow with a cast in his eye, and a green waistcoat. But I mean to stick to Wildfire: I shan't get a better one at a fence in a hurry. The mare's got more blood, but she's a bit too weak in the hindquarters."

Bryce of course guessed that Dunstan wanted to sell the horse, and Dunstan knew that he guessed it (horse-dealing is only one of many human transactions carried on in this ingenious manner). They both thought the bargain was in its first stage, when Bryce replied ironically, "I'm surprised you want to keep him, for I never heard of a man who didn't want to sell his horse if he got half again what the horse was worth. You'll be lucky if you get a hundred."

Keating rode up now, and the transaction became more complicated. It ended in the purchase of the horse by Bryce for a hundred and twenty, to be paid on the delivery of Wildfire, safe and sound, at the Batherley stables. It did occur to Dunsey that it might be wise for him to give up the day's hunting, proceed at once to Batherley, and, having waited for Bryce's return, hire a horse to carry him home with the money in his pocket. But the inclination for a run, encouraged by confidence in his luck, and by a drink of brandy from his pocket pistol at the conclusion of the bargain, was not easy to overcome, especially with a horse under him that would take the fences to everyone's admiration.

Dunstan, however, took one fence too many, and got his horse pierced with a hedge stake. Dunstan escaped without injury, but poor Wildfire, unconscious of his price, turned on his flank and painfully panted his last breath. A short time before, Dunstan had to get down to arrange his stirrup, which had made him fall behind, and so he had taken the fences more blindly. He was almost up with the hounds again when the fatal accident occurred. Dunstan no sooner recovered his legs, and saw that it was all over with Wildfire, than, with a little brandy and much swearing, he walked as fast as he could to a stand of trees. He planned to make his way to Batherley without encountering any member of the hunt. His first intention was to hire a horse there and ride home forthwith, for to walk many miles without a gun in his hand, and along an ordinary road, was out of the question. He did not much mind about taking the bad news to Godfrey, for he could also offer him the idea of Marner's money. If Godfrey kicked, as he always did, at the notion of making a fresh debt from which he himself got the smallest share, he wouldn't kick long. Dunstan felt sure he could worry Godfrey into anything. The idea of Marner's money became more vivid, now that it was needed. The prospect of appearing at Batherley with the muddy boots of a pedestrian, and facing the grinning queries of stablemen, seemed very unpleasant indeed. Moreover, he did not have enough money to cover his small debt to the stable keeper, without payment of which the man had declared he would never do any more business with Dunsey Cass. He was not so very much farther from home than he was from Batherley, but Dunsey, not being the clearest thinker, was only led to his decision by other reasons.

It was now nearly four o'clock, and a mist was gathering, so the sooner he got into the road the better. He remembered having crossed the road and seen the signpost only a little while before Wildfire broke down. Buttoning his coat, twisting the lash of his hunting whip compactly round the handle, and rapping the tops of his boots with a self-possessed air, as if to assure himself that he was not at all taken by surprise, he set off with the sense that he was undertaking a remarkable feat. When a young gentleman like Dunsey is reduced to so exceptional a mode of transportation as walking, a whip in his hand is a comforting accessory. As he went along through the gathering mist, he was always rapping his whip somewhere. It was Godfrey's whip, which he had chosen to take without asking because it had a gold handle. Of course, no one could see when Dunstan held it that the name Godfrey Cass was cut in deep letters on that gold handle. They could only see that it was a very handsome whip. Dunsey was not without fear that he might meet some acquaintance in whose eyes he would cut a pitiable figure, for mist is no screen when people get close to each other. But when he at last found himself in the well-known Raveloe lanes without having met a soul, he silently remarked that this was part of his usual good luck. But now the mist, helped by the evening darkness, was more of a screen than he desired, for it hid the ruts into which his feet were liable to slip. In fact, it hid everything, so that he had to guide his steps by dragging his whip along the low bushes in advance of the hedgerow. He must soon, he thought, be getting near the opening at the Stone Pits. He should find it by the break in the hedgerow. He found it, however, by certain gleams of light, which he guessed were from

Silas Marner's cottage. That cottage and the money hidden within it had been in his mind continually during his walk. He had been imagining ways of persuading and tempting the weaver to part with his money for the sake of receiving interest. Dunstan felt as if there must be a little bullying added to the persuading, for his own arithmetic was not clear enough to make a convincing argument. As for the issue of security, he regarded it as a means of cheating a man by making him believe that he would be paid. Dunstan had already decided that Godfrey would be sure to hand over the task to his more daring and cunning brother.

By the time he saw the light gleaming through the chinks of Marner's shutters, Dunstan was ready to talk to the weaver. There were several things he might get out of such a conversation: the weaver had possibly got a lantern, and Dunstan was tired of feeling his way. He was still nearly three-quarters of a mile from home, and the lane was becoming unpleasantly slippery, for the mist was passing into rain. He turned up the bank, not without some fear lest he might miss the right way, since he was not certain whether the light were in front or on the side of the cottage. But he felt the ground before him cautiously with his whip handle, and at last arrived safely at the door. He knocked loudly, rather enjoying the idea that the old fellow would be frightened at the sudden noise. But all was silent in the cottage. Had the weaver gone to bed, then? If so, why had he left a light? That was a strange forgetfulness in a miser. Dunstan knocked still more loudly, and, without pausing for a reply, pushed his fingers through the latch hole, intending to shake the door and pull the latch string up and down, not doubting that the door was fastened. But, to his surprise, at this double motion the door opened, and he found himself in front of a bright fire which lit up every corner of the cottage—the bed, the loom, the three chairs, and the table— and showed him that Marner was not there.

Nothing at that moment could be much more inviting to Dunsey than the bright fire on the brick hearth, and he seated himself by it at once. There was something in front of the fire, too, that would have been inviting to a hungry man, if it had been in a different stage of cooking. It was a small bit of pork suspended from the kettle hanger by a string passed through a large door key, in a way known to primitive housekeepers. But the pork had been hung at the farthest end of the hanger, apparently to prevent the pork from roasting too quickly during the owner's absence.

The old staring simpleton had hot meat for

his supper, thought Dunstan. People had always said he lived on moldy bread, on purpose to ruin his appetite. But where could he be at this time, and on such an evening, leaving his supper in this stage of preparation, and his door unfastened? Perhaps the weaver had gone outside his cottage to fetch in fuel, or for some such brief purpose, and had slipped into the Stone Pit. That was an interesting idea to Dunstan. If the weaver was dead, who had a right to his money? Who would know where his money was hidden? Who would know that anybody had come to take it away? The pressing question, "Where is the money?" now took such hold of him as to make him quite forget that the weaver's death was not certain.

There were only three hiding places where he had ever heard of cottagers' stashes being found: the thatch, the bed, and a hole in the floor. Marner's cottage had no thatch. Dunstan's first act was to go up to the bed. But while he did so, his eyes traveled eagerly over the floor, where the bricks, distinct in the firelight, were discernible under the sprinkling of sand. But there was one spot, and one only, that was quite covered with sand, and sand showing the marks of fingers, which had apparently been careful to spread it over a given space. It was near the treadles of the loom.

In an instant Dunstan darted to that spot, swept away the sand with his whip, and, inserting the thin end of the hook between the bricks, found that they were loose. In haste he lifted up two bricks, and saw what he had no doubt was the object of his search. For what could there be but money in those two leather bags? And, from their weight, they must be filled with guineas. Dunstan felt round the hole, to be certain that it held no more. Then he hastily replaced the bricks, and spread the sand over them.

Hardly more than five minutes had passed since he entered the cottage, but it seemed to Dunstan like a long while. He felt a vague dread laying hold on him, as he rose to his feet with the bags in his hand. He would hasten out into the darkness, and then consider what he should do with the bags. He closed the door behind him immediately. A few steps would be enough to carry him away from the light of the shutter chinks and the latch hole. The rain and darkness had got thicker, and he was glad of it, though it was awkward walking with both hands filled. But when he had gone a yard or two, he might take his time. So he stepped forward into the darkness.

Chapter 5

When Dunstan Cass turned his back on the cottage, Silas Marner was not more than a hundred yards away from it, plodding along from the village with a sack thrown round his shoulders as an overcoat, and with a lantern in his hand. His legs were weary, but his mind was at ease. Silas was thinking with double complacency of his supper: first, because it would be hot and savory, and secondly, because it would cost him nothing. For the little bit of pork was a present from that excellent housewife, Miss Priscilla Lammeter, to whom he had this day carried home a handsome piece of linen.

It was only on an occasion like this that Silas indulged himself with roast meat. Supper was his favorite meal, because it came at his time of revelry, when his heart warmed over his gold. Whenever he had roast meat, he always chose to have it for supper. But this evening, he had no sooner ingeniously knotted his string fast round his bit of pork, twisted the string over his door key, passed it through the handle, and made it fast on the hanger, than he remembered that a piece of very fine twine was indispensable to setting up a new piece of work in his loom early in the morning.

It had slipped his memory, because, in coming from Mr. Lammeter's, he had not had to pass through the village. But to lose time by going on errands in the morning was out of the question. It was a nasty fog to turn out into, but there were things Silas loved better than his own comfort. So, drawing his pork to the end of the hanger, and arming himself with his lantern and his old sack, he set out on what, in ordinary weather, would have been a twenty-minute errand. He could not have locked his door without undoing his well-knotted string and delaying his supper, and it was not worth his while to make that sacrifice. What thief would find his way to the stone pits on such a night as this? And why should he come on this particular night, when he had never come through all the fifteen years before?

He reached his door satisfied that his errand was done. He opened it, and to his shortsighted eyes everything remained as he had left it, except that the fire sent out a welcome increase of heat. He trod about the floor while setting down his lantern and throwing aside his hat and sack, so as to merge the marks of Dunstan's feet on the sand in the marks of his own nailed boots. Then he moved his pork nearer to the fire, and sat down to the agreeable business of tending the meat and warming himself at the same time.

Anyone who had looked at him as the red light shone upon his pale face, strange straining eyes, and meager body, would perhaps have understood the mixture of contemptuous pity, dread, and suspicion with which he was regarded by his neighbors in Raveloe. Yet few men could be more harmless than poor Marner. In his truthful simple soul, not even the growing greed and worship of gold could arouse any vice directly harmful to others. Without faith or affection, he had clung with all his might to his work and his money, and like all objects to which a man devotes himself, they had exerted their influence on him. His loom, as he worked on it without ceasing, had in its turn worked on him, and built his appetite for monotony. His gold, as he hung over it and saw it grow, gathered to it all his power of loving.

As soon as he was warm he began to think it would be a long while to wait till after supper before he drew out his guineas, and it would be pleasant to see them on the table before him as he ate his feast. Joy is the best of wine, and Silas's guineas were a golden wine of that sort. He rose and placed his candle unsuspectingly on the floor near his loom, swept away the sand without noticing any change, and removed the bricks. The sight of the empty hole made his heart leap violently, but the belief that his gold was gone could not come at once—only terror, and the eager effort to put an end to the terror.

He passed his trembling hand all about the hole, thinking that his eyes had deceived him. Then he held the candle in the hole and examined it curiously, trembling more and more. At last he shook so violently that he dropped the candle, and lifted his hands to his head, trying to steady himself, so that he might think. Had he put his gold somewhere else, by a sudden decision last night, and then forgotten it? A man falling into dark waters seeks a momentary footing even on sliding stones. Silas, by acting as if he believed in false hopes, warded off the moment of despair. He searched in every corner, he turned his bed over, and shook it, and kneaded it; he looked in his brick oven where he laid his sticks. When there was no other place to be searched, he kneeled down again and felt once more all round the hole. There was no place left to look. The gold was gone.

Again he put his trembling hands to his head, and gave a wild ringing scream, the cry of desolation. For a few moments after, he stood motionless; but the cry had relieved him from the first maddening pressure of the truth. He turned, and tottered toward his loom, and got into the seat where he worked, instinctively seeking this as the strongest assurance of reality.

And now that all the false hopes had vanished, and the first shock of certainty was past, the idea of a thief began to present itself, and he entertained it eagerly, because a thief might be caught and made to restore the gold. The thought brought some new strength with it, and he started from his loom to the door. As he opened it the rain beat in upon him, for it was falling more and more heavily. There were no footsteps to be tracked on such a night. When had the thief come? During Silas's absence in the daytime the door had been locked, and there had been no marks of any intruder. And in the evening, too, he said to himself, everything was the same as when he had left it. The sand and bricks looked as if they had not been moved.

Was it a thief who had taken the bags? Or was it a cruel power that no hands could reach, which had delighted in making him a second time desolate? He shrank from this idea, and fixed his mind with struggling effort on the robber who could be reached by hands. His thoughts turned to all the neighbors who had made any remarks, or asked any questions which he might now regard as a ground of suspicion. There was Jem Rodney, a known poacher, and otherwise disreputable. He had often met Marner in his journeys across the fields, and had said something in jest about the weaver's money. Indeed, he had once irritated Marner, by lingering at the fire when he called to light his pipe, instead of going about his business. Jem Rodney was the man. He could be found and made to restore the money. Marner did not want to punish him, but only to get back his gold, whose absence had left his soul like a forlorn traveler on an unknown desert. The robber must be caught.

Marner's ideas of legal authority were confused, but he felt that he must go and report his loss. The great people in the village—the clergyman, the constable, and Squire Cass—would make Jem Rodney, or somebody else, deliver up the stolen money. He rushed out in the rain, in the excitement of this hope, forgetting to cover his head, not caring to fasten his door, for he felt as if he had nothing left to lose. He ran swiftly, till his lack of breath compelled him to slow down just as he was entering the village at the turning close to the Rainbow.

The Rainbow, in Marner's view, was a luxurious place for rich and stout husbands, whose wives had excessive stores of linen. It was the place where he was likely to find the powers and dignities of Raveloe, and where he could most speedily make his loss public. He lifted the latch, and turned into the bright bar on the right, where the less lofty customers of the house were in the habit of assembling. The parlor on the left was reserved for the more select society, like Squire Cass. But the parlor was dark tonight, most of those customers being at Mrs. Osgood's birthday dance, as Godfrey Cass was. And as a result, the group on the seats in the bar was more numerous than usual. Several people, who would otherwise have been admitted into the parlor to be belittled and intimidated, were content this evening to take their spirits-and-water where they could themselves intimidate and belittle the company that called for beer.

Chapter 6

The conversation, which was at a high pitch of animation when Silas approached the door of the Rainbow, had, as usual, been slow and intermittent when the company first assembled. The pipes began to be puffed in a severe silence. The more important customers drank spirits and sat nearest the fire, staring at each other as if a bet were depending on the first man who winked. Meanwhile, the beer drinkers kept their eyelids down and rubbed their hands across their mouths, as if their drinks of beer were a funereal duty carried out with embarrassing sadness. At last Mr. Snell, the landlord, a man of a neutral disposition, accustomed to stand aloof from human differences as those of beings who were all alike in need of liquor, broke the silence, by saying in a doubtful tone to his cousin the butcher, "Some folks would say that was a fine beast you drove in yesterday, Bob."

The butcher, a jolly, smiling, red-haired man, was not disposed to answer rashly. He gave a few puffs before he spat and replied, "And they wouldn't be fur wrong, John."

After this feeble thaw, the silence set in as severely as before.

"Was it a red Durham?" said the ferrier, taking up the thread of discourse after the lapse of a few minutes. The ferrier looked at the landlord, and the landlord looked at the butcher, as the person who must take the responsibility of answering.

"Red it was," said the butcher, in his good-humored husky voice—"and a Durham it was."

"Then you needn't tell me who you bought it from," said the ferrier, looking round with some triumph. "I know who has got the red Durhams o' this countryside. And she'd a white star on her brow, I'll bet a penny?" The ferrier leaned forward with his hands on his knees as he put this question, and his eyes twinkled knowingly.

"Well; yes—she might," said the butcher, slowly, considering that he was giving a decided affirmative. "I don't say contrary."

"I knew that very well," said the ferrier, throwing himself backward again. "If I don't know Mr. Lammeter's cows, I should like to know who does—that's all. And as for the cow you've bought, bargain or no bargain, I know all the medicine she's had." The ferrier looked fierce, and the mild butcher's conversational spirit was roused a little.

"I'm not for contradicting no man," he said. "I'm for peace and quiet. All I say is, it's a lovely carcass—and anybody as was reasonable, it would bring tears into their eyes to look at it."

"Well, it's the cow I treated, whatever it is," pursued the ferrier, angrily. "And it was Mr. Lammeter's cow, else you told a lie when you said it was a red Durham."

"I tell no lies," said the butcher, with the same mild huskiness as before, "and I contradict no one—not if a man was to swear himself black. All I say is, it's a lovely carcass. And what I say, I'll stick to; but I'll quarrel with no man."

"No," said the ferrier, with bitter sarcasm, looking at the company generally. "And perhaps you aren't pigheaded; and perhaps you didn't say the cow was a red Durham; and perhaps you didn't say she'd got a star on her brow—stick to that, now you're at it."

"Come, come," said the landlord; "let the cow alone. The truth lies between you: you're both right and both wrong, as I always say. And as for the cow's being Mr. Lammeter's, I say nothing to that; but I say that the Rainbow's the Rainbow. And if the talk is to be o' the Lammeters, you know the most about that, eh, Mr. Macey? You remember when first Mr. Lammeter's father come into these parts, and took the Warrens?"

Mr. Macey, tailor and parish clerk, held his white head on one side, and twirled his thumbs with an air of complacency, slightly seasoned with criticism. He smiled pityingly, in answer to the landlord's appeal, and said, "Aye, aye; I know, I know; but I let other folks talk. I've given up to the young'uns. Ask them who have been to school at Tarley. They've learned how to speak."

"If you're pointing at me, Mr. Macey," said his deputy clerk, with an air of anxious propriety, "I'm not a man to speak out of my place. As the psalm says, 'I know what's right, nor only so, but also practice what I know.'"

"Well, then, I wish you'd keep hold o' the tune, when it's set for you. If you're for practicing, I wish you'd practice that," said a large jolly man, an excellent wheelwright during the week, but on Sundays leader of the choir. He winked, as he spoke, at two of the company, who were known officially as the "bassoon" and the "key bugle."

Mr. Tookey, the deputy clerk, who shared

the unpopularity common to deputies, turned very red, but replied, with careful moderation— "Mr. Winthrop, if you'll bring me any proof that I'm in the wrong, I'm ready to change. But some people have their own ears for a standard, and expect the whole choir to follow 'em. There may be two opinions, I hope."

"Aye, aye," said Mr. Macey, who felt very well satisfied with this attack on youthful presumption, "you're right there, Tookey. There's always two 'pinions. There's the 'pinion a man has of himself, and there's the 'pinion other folks have of him. There'd be two 'pinions about a cracked bell, if the bell could hear itself."

"Well, Mr. Macey," said poor Tookey, serious amidst the general laughter, "I undertook to partially fill the office of parish clerk on Mr. Crackenthorp's wishes. And it's one of the rights thereof to sing in the choir—what right do you have to sing in it?"

"Ah! But the old gentleman and you are different," said Ben Winthrop. "The old gentleman's got a gift. Why, the Squire used to invite him to take a glass, only to hear him sing the 'Red Rover,' didn't he, Mr. Macey? It's a natural gift. There's my little lad Aaron, he's got a gift—he can sing a tune off straight. But as for you, Master Tookey, you'd better stick to your

'Amens.' Your voice is good enough when you keep it up in your nose. It's your inside that isn't right made for music. It's no better than a hollow stalk."

This kind of unflinching frankness was the highest form of joke to the company at the Rainbow, and Ben Winthrop's insult was felt by everybody to have capped Mr. Macey's remarks.

"I see what it is plain enough," said Mr. Tookey, unable to keep cool any longer. "There's a conspiracy to turn me out o' the choir, as I shouldn't share the Christmas money—that's where it is. But I shall speak to Mr. Crackenthorp. I'll not be put upon by no man."

"Nay, nay, Tookey," said Ben Winthrop. "We'll pay you your share to keep out of it— that's what we'll do. There's things folks would pay to be rid of, besides vermin."

"Come, come," said the landlord, who felt that paying people for their absence was a principle dangerous to society. "A joke's a joke. We're all good friends here, I hope. We must give and take. You're both right and you're both wrong, as I say. I agree with Mr. Macey here, as there's two opinions. If mine was asked, I should say they're both right. Tookey's right and Winthrop's right, and they've only got to split the difference and make themselves even."

The ferrier was puffing his pipe rather

fiercely, in some contempt at this trivial discussion. He had no ear for music himself, and never went to church, being of the medical profession, and likely to be needed for delicate cows. But the butcher, having music in his soul, had listened with a divided desire for Tookey's defeat and for the preservation of the peace.

"To be sure," he said, following up the landlord's conciliatory view. "We're fond of our old clerk. It's natural, and him used to be such a singer, and got a brother known as the first fiddler in this countryside. Eh, it's a pity that Solomon doesn't live in our village, and could give us a tune when we liked; eh, Mr. Macey? I'd keep him in liver and lights for nothing—that I would."

"Aye, aye," said Mr. Macey. "Our family's been known for musicians as far back as anybody can tell. But them things are dying out, as I tell Solomon every time he comes round. There's no voices like what there used to be, and there's nobody remembers what we remember, if it isn't the old crows."

"Aye, you remember when first Mr. Lammeter's father come into these parts, don't you, Mr. Macey?" said the landlord.

"I should think I did," said the old man, who had now gone through that complimentary process necessary to bring him up to the point of narration. "A fine old gentleman he was—as fine as, and finer than Mr. Lammeter now is. He came from a bit north, so far as I could ever make out. But there's nobody rightly knows about those parts. But he brought a fine breed o' sheep with him, so there must be pastures there, and everything reasonable. We heard that he'd sold his own land to come and take the Warrens, and that seemed odd for a man that had land of his own, to come and rent a farm in a strange place. But they said it was because of his wife's dying. Anyhow, we soon saw we'd got a new parish'ner that knew the rights and customs o' things, and kept a good house, and was well looked on by everybody. And the young man—that's the Mr. Lammeter that now is—soon begun to court Miss Osgood, that's the sister o' the Mr. Osgood as now is, and a fine handsome lass she was—eh, you can't think—they pretend this young lass is like her, but that's the way wi' people that don't know what come before 'em. I should know, for I helped the old rector, Mr. Drumlow it was, I helped him marry 'em."

Here Mr. Macey paused. He always gave his narrative in installments, expecting to be questioned according to precedent.

"Aye, and a particular thing happened, didn't it, Mr. Macey, so that you were likely to remember that marriage?" said the landlord, in a congratulatory tone.

"I should think there did—a very particular thing," said Mr. Macey, nodding sideways. "For Mr. Drumlow—poor old gentleman, I was fond of him, though he'd got a bit confused in his head, what wi' age and wi' taking a drop o' something warm when the service was on a cold morning. And young Mr. Lammeter, he must be married in January, which, to be sure, is an unreasonable time to be married in, for it isn't like a christening or a burying, that you can't help. So Mr. Drumlow—poor old gentleman, I was fond of him—but when he come to put the questions, he put 'em wrong. He says, 'Wilt thou have this man to be thy wedded wife?' says he, and then he says, 'Wilt thou have this woman to be thy wedded husband?' But the strangest thing of all was that nobody took any notice of it but me, and they answered straight off 'yes,' without listening to what went before."

"But you knew what was going on well enough, didn't you, Mr. Macey? You were awake enough, eh?" said the butcher.

"Lord bless you!" said Mr. Macey, pausing, "why, I was all a-tremble: it was as if I'd been a coat pulled by the two tails, like. For I couldn't stop the parson, I couldn't take upon me to do that. Yet I said to myself, I says, "Suppose they shouldn't be fast married, 'cause the words are wrong?" and my head went working like a mill, for I was always turning things over and seeing all round 'em. I says to myself, "Is't the meanin' or the words as makes folks fast i' wedlock?" For the parson meant right, and the bride and bridegroom meant right. But then, when I come to think on it, meanin' goes but a little way i' most things, for you may mean to stick things together and your glue may be bad, and then where are you? And so I says to myself, "It isn't the meanin', it's the glue." And I was as worried as if I'd got three bells to pull at once, when we went into the vestry, and they begun to sign their names. But where's the use o' talking? You can't think what goes on in a man's inside."

"But you held it in for all that, didn't you, Mr. Macey?" said the landlord.

"Aye, I held in tight till I was by myself with Mr. Drumlow, and then I came out with everything, but respectful, as I always did. And he made light of it, and he says, "Pooh, pooh, Macey, make yourself easy," he says. "It's neither the meaning nor the words—it's the register does it—that's the glue." So you see he settled it easy, for parsons and doctors know everything by heart, like, so as they aren't worried with thinking what's the rights and wrongs o' things, as I been many and many's the time. And sure enough the wedding turned out all right, only poor Mrs. Lammeter—that's Miss Osgood as was—died afore the lasses was growed up. But for prosperity and everything respectable, there's no family more looked on."

Every one of Mr. Macey's audience had heard this story many times, but it was listened to as if it had been a favorite tune, and at certain points the puffing of the pipes was momentarily suspended, that the listeners might give their whole minds to the expected words. But there was more to come, and Mr. Snell, the landlord, duly put the leading question.

"Why, old Mr. Lammeter had a pretty fortune, didn't they say, when he come into these parts?"

"Well, yes," said Mr. Macey, "but I daresay this Mr. Lammeter's worked hard to keep it whole. For there was always talk that nobody could get rich on the Warrens, though he holds it cheap, for it's what they call Charity Land."

"Aye, and there's few folks know so well as you how it come to be Charity Land, eh, Mr. Macey?" said the butcher.

"How should they?" said the old clerk, with some contempt. "Why, my grandfather made the grooms' livery for that Mr. Cliff who came and built the big stables at the Warrens. Why, they're stables four times as big as Squire Cass's, for he thought o' nothing but horses and hunting. Cliff was a London tailor, some folks said, as had gone mad with cheating. For he couldn't ride; lord bless you! They said he'd got no more grip o' the horse than if his legs had been cross sticks.

"My grandfather heard old Squire Cass say so many and many a time. But ride he would, as if Old Harry had been a-driving him. He'd a son, a lad o' sixteen; and nothing would his father have him do, but he must ride and ride— though the lad was frightened, they said. And it was a common saying that the father wanted to ride the tailor out o' the lad, and make a gentle-man of him. I'm a tailor myself, and since God made me such, I'm proud of it, for 'Macey, Tailor,' has been wrote up over our door since afore the Queen's head went out on the shillings. But Cliff, he was ashamed o' being called a tailor, and he was sore vexed that his rid-ing was laughed at, and the gentlefolks here-about could not abide him. However, the poor lad got sickly and died, and the father didn't live long after him, for he got queerer than ever, and they said he used to go out i' the dead o' the night, with a lantern in his hand, to the stables, and set a lot o' lights burning, for he got as he couldn't sleep.

"There he'd stand, cracking his whip and

looking at his horses. They said it was a mercy that the stables didn't get burnt down wi' the poor dumb creatures in 'em. But at last he died raving, and they found as he'd left all his property, Warrens and all, to a London Charity, and that's how the Warrens come to be Charity Land. Though, as for the stables, Mr. Lammeter never uses 'em. If you was to set the doors a-banging in 'em, it would sound like thunder over half the parish."

"Aye, but there's more going on in the stables than what folks see by daylight, eh, Mr. Macey?" said the landlord.

"Aye, aye; go that way of a dark night, that's all," said Mr. Macey, winking mysteriously, "and then make believe, if you like, that you didn't see lights i' the stables, nor hear the stamping o' the horses, nor the cracking o' the whips, and howling, too, if it's toward daybreak. 'Cliff's Holiday' has been the name of it ever since I were a boy. Some said it was the holiday Old Harry gave him from roasting. That's what my father told me, and he was a reasonable man, though there's folks nowadays know what happened afore they were born better than they know their own business."

"What do you say to that, eh, Dowlas?" said the landlord, turning to the ferrier, who was swelling with impatience for his cue. "There's a nut for you to crack."

Mr. Dowlas was the negative spirit in the company, and was proud of his position.

"Say? I say what a man should say that doesn't shut his eyes to look at a signpost. I say I'm ready to wager any man ten pound, if he'll stand out wi' me any dry night in the pasture before the Warren stables, as we shall neither see lights nor hear noises, if it isn't the blowing of our own noses. That's what I say, and I've said it many a time. But there's nobody who will venture a ten-pound note on their ghosts that they're so sure of."

"Why, Dowlas, that's easy betting, that is," said Ben Winthrop. "You might as well bet a man as he wouldn't catch rheumatism if he stood up to his neck in the pool of a frosty night. It would be fine fun for a man to win his bet that he'd catch rheumatism. Folks that believe in Cliff's Holiday aren't agoing to venture near it for a matter o' ten pound."

"If Master Dowlas wants to know the truth on it," said Mr. Macey, with a sarcastic smile, tapping his thumbs together, "he doesn't have to lay any bet. Let him go and stand by himself—there's nobody who will stop him. Then he can let the parish'ners know if they're wrong."

"Thank you! I'm obliged to you," said the

ferrier, with a snort of scorn. "If folks are fools, it's no business o' mine. I don't want to make out the truth about ghosts. I know it already. But I'm not against a bet—everything fair and open. Let any man bet me ten pound that I shall see Cliff's Holiday, and I'll go and stand by myself. I want no company. I'd as soon do it as I'd fill this pipe."

"Ah, but who's to watch you, Dowlas, and see you do it? That's no fair bet," said the butcher.

"No fair bet?" replied Mr. Dowlas, angrily. "I should like to hear any man stand up and say I want to bet unfair. Come now, Master Lundy, I should like to hear you say it."

"Very like you would," said the butcher. "But it's no business o' mine. You're none o' my bargains, and I aren't a-going to try and debate your price. If anybody will bid for you at your own value, let him. I'm for peace and quietness, I am."

"Yes, that's what every yapping cur is, when you hold a stick up at him," said the ferrier. "But I'm afraid o' neither man nor ghost, and I'm ready to lay a fair bet. I aren't a turn-tail cur."

"Aye, but there's this in it, Dowlas," said the landlord, speaking in a tone of much candor and tolerance. "There's folks, in my opinion, they can't see ghosts, not if they stood as plain as a pike staff before 'em. And there's reason for that. For there's my wife, now, can't smell, not if she'd the strongest o' cheese under her nose. I never seen a ghost myself; but then I says to myself, *Very like I haven't got the smell for 'em.* And so, I'm for holding with both sides, for, as I say, the truth lies between 'em. And if Dowlas was to go and stand, and say he'd never seen a wink o' Cliff's Holiday all the night through, I'd back him. And if anybody said that Cliff's Holiday was certain sure, for all that, I'd back him too. For the smell's what I go by."

The landlord's argument was not well received by the ferrier—a man intensely opposed to compromise. "Tut, tut," he said, setting down his glass with refreshed irritation. "What's the smell got to do with it? Did ever a ghost give a man a black eye? That's what I should like to know. If ghosts want me to believe in 'em, let 'em leave off skulking in the dark and in lonely places—let 'em come where there's company and candles."

"As if ghosts would want to be believed in by anybody so ignorant!" said Mr. Macey, in deep disgust at the ferrier's inability to understand the conditions of ghostly phenomena.

Chapter 7

Yet the next moment there seemed to be some evidence that ghosts had a more accommodating nature than Mr. Macey thought. The pale thin figure of Silas Marner was suddenly seen standing in the warm light, uttering no word, but looking round at the company with his strange unearthly eyes. The men's long pipes all moved at once, like the antennae of startled insects, and every man present, even the skeptical ferrier, had an impression that he saw, not Silas Marner in the flesh, but a ghost.

The door by which Silas had entered was hidden by the high-screened seats, and no one had noticed his approach. Mr. Macey, sitting a long way from the ghost, was probably feeling triumphant. Had he not always said that when

Silas Marner was in that strange trance of his, his soul went loose from his body? Here was the proof. Nevertheless, on the whole, he would have been happy without it. For a few moments there was a dead silence, since Marner was too worked up to speak. The landlord, who always wanted to keep his house open to everyone, at last addressed the ghost.

"Master Marner," he said, in a friendly tone, "what's your business here?"

"Robbed!" said Silas, gaspingly. "I've been robbed! I want the constable—and the Justice—and Squire Cass—and Mr. Crackenthorp."

"Get hold of him, Jem Rodney," said the landlord, the idea of a ghost subsiding. "He's off his head. He's wet through."

Jem Rodney was the outermost man, and sat conveniently near Marner's standing place. But he declined to give his services.

"Come and get hold of him yourself, Mr. Snell, if you've a mind," said Jem, rather sullenly. "He's been robbed, and murdered too, for all I know," he added, in a muttering tone.

"Jem Rodney!" said Silas, turning and fixing his strange eyes on the suspected man.

"Aye, Master Marner, what do you want wi' me?" said Jem, trembling a little, and seizing his drinking can as a defensive weapon.

"If it was you who stole my money," said

Silas, clasping his hands entreatingly, and raising his voice to a cry, "give it back—and I won't meddle with you. I won't set the constable on you. Give it back, and I'll let you—I'll let you have a guinea."

"Me stole your money!" said Jem, angrily. "I'll pitch this can at your eye if you talk o' my stealing your money."

"Come, come, Master Marner," said the landlord, now rising resolutely, and seizing Marner by the shoulder, "if you've got any information, say it calmly, and show that you're in your right mind, if you expect anybody to listen to you. You're as wet as a drowned rat. Sit down and dry yourself, and speak."

"Ah, to be sure, man," said the ferrier, who began to feel that he had not risen to the occasion. "Let's have no more staring and screaming, else we'll have you strapped for a madman. That was why I didn't speak at first—I thought the man's run mad."

"Aye, aye, make him sit down," said several voices at once, well pleased that the reality of ghosts remained still an open question.

The landlord forced Marner to take off his coat, and then to sit down on a chair away from everyone else, in the center of the circle and in the direct rays of the fire. The weaver, too feeble to have any distinct purpose beyond that of getting help to recover his money, submitted unresistingly. The fears of the company were now forgotten in their strong curiosity, and all faces were turned toward Silas. The landlord, having seated himself again, said, "Now then, Master Marner, what's this you've got to say— that you've been robbed? Speak out."

"He'd better not say again that it was me robbed him," cried Jem Rodney, hastily. "What could I ha' done with his money? I could as easy steal the parson's robe, and wear it."

"Hold your tongue, Jem, and let's hear what he's got to say," said the landlord. "Now then, Master Marner."

Silas now told his story, under frequent questioning as the mysterious nature of the robbery became evident. This strange situation of opening his trouble to his Raveloe neighbors, of sitting in the warmth of a hearth not his own, and feeling the presence of faces and voices that were his nearest promise of help, had an influence on Marner, in spite of his passionate worry over his loss. Our consciousness rarely notices the beginning of a growth within us anymore than outside us: the sap has been flowing long before we detect the smallest sign of the bud.

His audience soon lost their slight suspicion of him, for it was impossible for the neighbors to doubt that Marner was telling the truth, because, as Mr. Macey observed, "Folks that had the devil behind them were not likely to be so mushed" as poor Silas was. By the strange fact that the robber had left no trace, and had happened to know the moment, unknowable by mere mortals, when Silas would go away from home without locking his door, it seemed likely that this crime had been done by somebody it was no use to set the constable after. Why this supernatural felon should have to wait till the door was left unlocked, was a question which nobody asked.

"It wasn't Jem Rodney, Master Marner," said the landlord. "You mustn't be looking at poor Jem. There may be a bit of an account against Jem for the matter of a hare or so, if anybody was to keep their eyes staring open, and never to wink. But Jem's been a-sitting here drinking his can, like the most decent man i' the parish, since before you left your house, Master Marner."

"Aye, aye," said Mr. Macey. "Let's not accuse the innocent. That isn't the law. Let's have no accusing o' the innocent, Master Marner."

Memory was not so utterly asleep in Silas that it could not be awakened by these words. With a feeling of regret as new and strange to him as everything else within the last hour, he started from his chair and went up to Jem. "I was wrong," he said. "Yes, yes—I ought to have thought. There's nothing to witness against you, Jem. Only you'd been into my house oftener than anybody else, and so you came into my head. I don't accuse you—I won't accuse anybody—only," he added, lifting up his hands to his head, and turning away with bewildered misery, "I try—I try to think where my guineas can be."

"Aye, aye, they're gone where it's hot enough to melt 'em, I bet," said Mr. Macey.

"Tchuh!" said the ferrier. And then he asked, with a cross-examining air, "How much money might there be in the bags, Master Marner?"

"Two hundred and seventy-two pounds, twelve and sixpence, last night when I counted it," said Silas, seating himself again, with a groan.

"Pooh! Why, they wouldn't be so heavy to carry. Some tramp's been in, that's all. As for the no footmarks, and the bricks and the sand being all right—why, your eyes are pretty much like a insect's, Master Marner. They're obliged to look so close, you can't see much at a time. It's my opinion that, if I'd been you, I wouldn't have thought I'd found everything as I left it. But what I vote is, that two of the most sensible men go with you to Master Kench, the constable's—he's ill i' bed, I know that much—and get him to appoint one of us his deputy. That's the law, and I don't think anybody will contradict me.

"It isn't much of a walk to Kench's. If it's me that is deputy, I'll go back with you, Master Marner, and examine your premises. If anybody's got any fault to find with that, I'll thank him to stand up and say it out like a man."

By this speech the ferrier had re-established his self-importance, and waited with confidence to hear himself named as one of the most sensible men.

"Let us see how the night is, though," said the landlord, who also considered himself important in the matter. "Why, it rains heavy still," he said, returning from the door.

"Well, I'm not the man to be afraid o' the rain," said the ferrier. "For it'll look bad when Justice Malam hears that respectable men like us had information laid before 'em and took no steps."

The landlord agreed with this view, and after taking the sense of the company, he consented to go to Kench's. But to the ferrier's strong disgust, Mr. Macey now objected to his proposing himself as a deputy-constable. That wise old gentleman, claiming to know the law, stated that no doctor could be a constable.

"And you're a doctor, I reckon, though you're only a cow doctor. A fly's a fly, though it may be a horsefly," concluded Mr. Macey, wondering a little at his own cuteness.

There was a hot debate upon this, the ferrier being of course reluctant to deny being a doctor, but contending that a doctor could be a constable if he liked. The law meant, he said, that he needn't be one if he didn't like. Mr. Macey thought this was nonsense, since the law was not likely to be fonder of doctors than of other folks. Moreover, if it was in the nature of doctors more than of other men not to like being constables, how came Mr. Dowlas to be so eager to act in that capacity?

"I don't want to act the constable," said the ferrier, driven into a corner by this merciless reasoning. "There's no man who can truthfully say I do. But if there's to be any jealousy about going to Kench's in the rain, let them go who want to—you won't get me to go, I can tell you."

However, the landlord soon cleared up the dispute. Mr. Dowlas consented to go as a second person, who would not act officially. So poor Silas, furnished with some old coverings, went with his two companions into the rain again, thinking of the long night hours before him.

Chapter 8

When Godfrey Cass returned from Mrs. Osgood's party at midnight, he was not surprised to learn that Dunsey had not come home. Perhaps he had not sold Wildfire, and was waiting for another chance. Perhaps, on that foggy afternoon, he had preferred staying at the Red Lion at Batherley for the night, if the hunt had kept him in that neighborhood. After all, he was not likely to be concerned about leaving his brother in suspense. Godfrey's mind was too full of Nancy Lammeter's looks and behavior, too full of exasperation with himself, which the sight of her always produced in him, to give much thought to Wildfire, or to Dunstan's conduct.

The next morning the whole village was excited by the story of the robbery, and

Godfrey, like everyone else, discussed it and visited the Stone Pits. The rain had washed away all possible footprints, but a close investigation of the spot had revealed, in the direction away from the village, a tinderbox, with a flint and steel, half sunk in the mud. It was not Silas's tinderbox, for the only one he had ever had was still standing on his shelf. It was generally thought that the tinderbox in the ditch was somehow connected with the robbery.

A small minority shook their heads, and said that tinderboxes wouldn't solve the case, because Master Marner's tale had a queer look to it. They also said that it was known for a man to do himself a mischief, and then set the justice to look for the culprit. But when questioned closely as to their grounds for this opinion, and what Master Marner had to gain by such false pretences, they only shook their heads as before, observing that there was no knowing what some folks would do.

Moreover, they said everybody had a right to their own opinions, grounds or no grounds, and that the weaver, as everybody knew, was partly crazy. Mr. Macey, though he said Marner was telling the truth, also pooh-poohed the tinderbox. Indeed, he rejected it as a rather disrespectful suggestion implying that everything must be done by human hands. Nevertheless, he turned rather sharply on Mr. Tookey, when the zealous deputy carried it still farther, and doubted whether it was right to inquire into a robbery at all when the circumstances were so mysterious.

"As if," concluded Mr. Tookey, "As if there was nothing but what could be made out by justices and constables."

"Now, don't you overshoot the mark, Tookey," said Mr. Macey, shaking his head admonishingly. "That's what you're always doing. If I throw a stone and hit, you think there's something better than hitting, and you try to throw a stone beyond. What I said was against the tinderbox. I said nothing against justices and constables, for they're o' King George's making, and it wouldn't do for a man in a parish office to fly out against King George."

While these discussions were going on outside the Rainbow, a higher one was going on within, under the direction of Mr. Crackenthorp, the rector, assisted by Squire Cass and other important parishioners. It had just occurred to Mr. Snell, the landlord—he being, as he observed, a man accustomed to put two and two together—to connect the tinderbox with a peddler who had called to drink at the Rainbow about a month before, and had carried a tinderbox to light his pipe. Here, surely, was a clue to be followed. And since memory, when jostled with certain facts, is sometimes surprisingly active, Mr. Snell gradually recovered a vivid impression of the peddler's face and conversation. He had had an "unpleasant" look in his eye. To be sure, he didn't say anything particular—no, except that about the tinderbox—but it isn't what a man says, it's the way he says it. More-over, he had a dark foreign complexion, which hinted at dishonesty.

"Did he wear earrings?" Mr. Crackenthorp wished to know, having some acquaintance with foreign customs.

"Well—wait—let me see," said Mr. Snell. After stretching the corners of his mouth and contracting his eyes, as if he were trying to see the earrings, he appeared to give up, and said, "Well, he'd got earrings in his box to sell, so it's natural to suppose he might wear 'em. But he called at every house, almost, in the village. There's somebody else, maybe, saw 'em in his ears, though I can't rightly say."

Mr. Snell was correct that somebody else would remember the peddler's earrings. The news spread among the villagers that the parson had wanted to know whether the peddler wore earrings in his ears, and an impression was creat-ed that a great deal depended on this question. Of course, everyone who heard the question, not having any distinct image of the peddler as without earrings, immediately had an image of him with earrings, larger or smaller, as the case might be. The image then became a vivid recollection, so that the glazier's wife, a well-intentioned woman not given to lying, and whose house was among the cleanest in the village, was ready to declare that she had seen big earrings in the shape of the young moon, in the peddler's ears. Meanwhile, Jinny Oates, the cobbler's daughter, being a more imaginative person, stated not only that she had seen them too, but that they had made her blood creep.

Also, to further understand this clue of the tinderbox, a collection was made of everything purchased from the peddler at various houses, and carried to the Rainbow to be examined. In fact, there was a general feeling that the investigation should be done at the Rainbow, and that no man need offer his wife an excuse for going there while it was the scene of severe public duties.

Some disappointment was felt that Silas Marner remembered nothing about the peddler than that he had called at his door. He had not entered his house, having turned away at once when Silas had said that he wanted nothing. But Silas still clutched strongly at the idea of the peddler's being the culprit, if only because it gave him a definite image of the whereabouts of his gold: he could see it now in the peddler's box. The villagers observed that anybody but a "blind creature" like Marner would have seen the man prowling about, for how did he leave his tinderbox in the ditch close by, if he hadn't been lingering there? Doubtless, he had made his observations when he saw Marner at the door. Anybody might know by looking at him that the weaver was a half-crazy miser. It was a wonder the peddler hadn't murdered him. Men of that sort, with rings in their ears, had been known to murder often. There had been one tried for it recently enough for some people to remember.

Godfrey Cass, indeed, had treated it lightly, stating that he himself had bought a penknife from the peddler, and thought him a merry grinning fellow. It was all nonsense, he said, about the man's evil looks. But this was said to be the random talk of youth, "as if it was only Mr. Snell who had seen something odd about the peddler!" On the contrary, there were at least a half dozen who were ready to go before Justice Malam, and give much more striking testimony than any the landlord could furnish. It was to be hoped Mr. Godfrey would not go to Tarley and throw cold water on what Mr. Snell said there, and so prevent the justice from drawing up a warrant. Mr. Godfrey was suspected of this, when he was seen setting off on horseback in the direction of Tarley.

But by this time Godfrey's interest in the robbery had faded before his growing anxiety about Dunstan and Wildfire, and he was going, not to Tarley, but to Batherley, unable to rest in uncertainty about them any longer. The possibility that Dunstan had ridden away with Wildfire, to return when he had gambled away or otherwise squandered the price of the horse, was a fear greater than the thought of an accidental injury. Now that the dance at Mrs. Osgood's was past, he was irritated that he had trusted his horse to Dunstan. Instead of trying to calm his fears, he encouraged them, under that superstition that if we expect evil very strongly it is the less likely to come. When he heard a horse approaching at a trot, and saw a hat rising above a hedge beyond an angle of the lane, he felt as if his tactics had succeeded. But no sooner did the horse come within sight, than his heart sank again. It was not Wildfire, and the rider was not Dunstan, but Bryce, wearing a disagreeable expression.

"Well, Mr. Godfrey, that's a lucky brother of yours, that Master Dunsey, isn't he?"

"What do you mean?" said Godfrey, hastily.

"Why, hasn't he been home yet?" said Bryce.

"Home? No. What has happened? Be quick. What has he done with my horse?"

"Ah, I thought it was yours, though he pretended you had given it to him."

"Has he thrown him down and broken his knees?" said Godfrey, flushed with exasperation.

"Worse than that," said Bryce. "You see, I'd made a bargain with him to buy the horse for a hundred and twenty—a swinging price, but I always liked the horse. And what does he do but go and stake him—fly at a hedge with stakes in it, on top of a bank with a ditch before it. The horse had been dead a pretty good while when he was found. So Master Dunsey hasn't been home since, has he?"

"Home? No," said Godfrey, "and he'd better keep away. Confound me for a fool! I might have known this would be the end of it."

"Well, to tell you the truth," said Bryce, "after I'd bargained for the horse, it did come into my head that he might be riding and selling the horse without your knowledge, for I didn't believe it was his own. I knew Master Dunsey got up to his tricks sometimes. But where can he be? He hasn't been seen at Batherley. He couldn't have been hurt, for he must have walked off."

"Hurt?" said Godfrey, bitterly. "He'll never be hurt—he's made to hurt other people."

"Did you tell him to sell the horse?" said Bryce.

"Yes, I wanted to part with the horse—he

was always too hard in the mouth for me," said Godfrey. His pride ached at the thought that Bryce might guess the sale to be a matter of necessity. "I was going to see after him—I thought some mischief had happened. I'll go back now," he added, turning the horse's head, and wishing he could get rid of Bryce. He felt that the long-dreaded crisis in his life was close upon him. "You're coming on to Raveloe, aren't you?"

"Well, no, not now," said Bryce. "I was coming round there, for I had to go to Flitton, and I thought I might as well take you in my way, and just let you know about the horse. I suppose Master Dunsey doesn't like to show himself till the ill news had blown over a bit. He's perhaps gone to pay a visit at the Three Crowns, by Whitbridge—I know he's fond of the place."

"Perhaps he is," said Godfrey, rather absently. Then rousing himself, he said, with an effort at carelessness, "We shall hear of him soon enough, I'll be bound."

"Well, here's my turning," said Bryce, not surprised that Godfrey was rather down. "So I'll bid you good day, and wish I may bring you better news another time."

Godfrey rode along slowly, imagining the scene of confession to his father from which he felt that there was now no longer any escape. He must tell him about the money the very next morning. If he withheld the rest, Dunstan would be sure to come back shortly, and, finding that he must bear the brunt of his father's anger, would tell the whole story out of spite, even though he had nothing to gain by it. There was one step, perhaps, by which he might still win Dunstan's silence and put off the evil day: he might tell his father that he had himself spent the money paid to him by Fowler. Since he had never been guilty of such an offence before, the affair would blow over after a little storming. But Godfrey could not bend himself to this. He felt that in letting Dunstan have the money, he had already been as guilty as if he had spent the money directly for himself. Yet there was a distinction between the two acts that made him feel that the one was so much worse than the other as to be intolerable to him.

"I don't pretend to be a good fellow," he said to himself. "But I'm not a scoundrel—at least, I'll stop short somewhere. I'll bear the consequences of what I have done sooner than pretend that I've done something I never would. I'd never have spent the money for my own pleasure—I was tortured into it."

Through the remainder of this day Godfrey was set on telling his father everything, and so he decided to withhold the story of Wildfire's loss till the next morning, that it might serve as an introduction to more serious matters. The old Squire was used to his son's frequent absence from home, and thought neither Dunstan's nor Wildfire's non-appearance a matter calling for remark. Godfrey said to himself again and again, that if he let slip this one opportunity of confession, he might never have another. The revelation might be made in a more terrible way than by Dunstan's mischief—she might come as she had threatened to do. And then he tried to make the scene easier to himself by rehearsal. He made up his mind how he would pass from the admission of his weakness in letting Dunstan have the money to the fact that Dunstan had a hold on him that he had been unable to shake off, and how he would work up his father to expect something very bad before he told him the fact.

The old Squire was an unbending man. He made resolutions in violent anger, and he was not to be moved from them after his anger had subsided. Like many violent and implacable men, he allowed evils to grow out of his own neglect, till they pressed upon him with exasperating force, and then he turned round with fierce severity and became unrelentingly hard. This was his system with his tenants: he allowed them to get behind with rent, neglect their fences, reduce their stock, sell their straw, and otherwise go the wrong way. Then, when he became short of money because of this indulgence, he took the hardest measures and would listen to no appeal. Godfrey knew all this because he had constantly suffered annoyance from witnessing his father's sudden fits of stubbornness, which, given his own indecisive nature, he did not understand. Still, there was just the chance, Godfrey thought, that his father's pride might induce him to hush up the marriage, rather than throw his son out and make the family the talk of the country for ten miles round.

This was the strategy that Godfrey held in his mind till midnight, and he went to sleep thinking that he had finished debating. But when he awoke in the still morning darkness he found it impossible to reawaken his evening thoughts. Instead of arguments for confession, he could now see nothing but its evil consequences. The old dread of disgrace came back, and the dread of a barrier between himself and Nancy. He felt his old desire to rely on lucky chance to save him. Why, after all, should he cut off the hope of luck on purpose? He had seen the matter in a wrong light yesterday. He had been in a rage with Dunstan, and had thought of nothing but separating from him. But it would be wisest to try and soften his father's anger against Dunsey, and keep things as nearly as possible in their old condition. If Dunsey did not come back for a few days (and Godfrey did not know if the rascal had enough money in his pocket to keep away still longer), everything might blow over.

Chapter 9

Godfrey rose and had breakfast earlier than usual, but lingered in the parlor till his younger brothers had finished their meal and left. He awaited his father, who always took a walk with his managing-man before breakfast. Everyone breakfasted at a different hour in the Red House, and the Squire was always the latest, trying to work up his weak morning appetite. The table had been laid nearly two hours before he showed—a tall, stout man of sixty, with a knit brow and hard glance but a slack and feeble mouth. His clothes were disheveled, yet there was something distinguished about him, born of the self-possession and authority that come from serving no one. The Squire had been used to commanding respect all his life, used to the idea that his family, his tankards, and everything that was his, were the oldest and best. Since he never associated with any gentry higher than himself, his opinion was not disturbed by comparison.

He glanced at his son as he entered the room, and said, "What, sir! Haven't you had your breakfast yet?" There was no pleasant morning greeting between them—not because of any unfriendliness, but because the sweet flower of courtesy does not grow in such homes as the Red House.

"Yes, sir," said Godfrey, "I've had my breakfast, but I was waiting to speak to you."

"Ah! Well," said the Squire, throwing himself indifferently into his chair, and speaking in a coughing fashion, while he cut a piece of beef, and held it up before the deer hound that had come in with him. "Ring the bell for my ale, will you? You youngsters are concerned with your own pleasure, mostly. There's no hurry about it for anybody but yourselves."

The Squire's life was quite as idle as his sons', but it was a fiction kept up by himself and his contemporaries that youth was full of nothing but folly. Godfrey waited until the ale had been brought and the door closed—an interval during which Fleet, the deer hound, had consumed enough bits of beef to make a poor man's holiday dinner.

"There's been a cursed piece of bad luck

with Wildfire," he began. "Happened the day before yesterday."

"What! Broke his knees?" said the Squire, after taking a drink of ale. "I thought you knew how to ride better than that, sir. I never threw a horse down in my life. If I had, I might have only whistled for another, for my father wasn't quite so ready to spend as most, including myself. But I must turn over a new leaf. What with mortgages and debts, I'm as short o' cash as a roadside pauper. And that fool Kimble says the newspaper's talking about peace. Why, the country wouldn't have a leg to stand on. Prices would run down, and I should never get my rents, not if I turned all the fellows in. And there's that damned Fowler, I won't put up with him any longer. I've told Winthrop to go to Cox this very day. The lying scoundrel told me he'd be sure to pay me a hundred last month. He takes advantage because he's on that outlying farm, and thinks I shall forget him."

The Squire had delivered this speech in a coughing and interrupted manner, but with no pause long enough for Godfrey to jump in. He felt that his father meant to ward off any request for money, and that the emphasis he had put on his shortness of cash would probably put him in a bad state of mind to hear the rest of Godfrey's news. But he must go on, now he had begun.

"It's worse than breaking the horse's knees—he's been staked and killed," he said, as soon as his father was silent, and had begun to cut his meat. "But I wasn't thinking of asking you to buy me another horse. I was only thinking I'd lost the means of paying you with the price of Wildfire, as I'd meant to do. Dunsey took him to the hunt to sell him for me the other day, and after he'd made a bargain for a hundred and twenty with Bryce, he went after the hounds, and took some fool's leap that killed the horse at once. If it hadn't been for that, I should have paid you a hundred pounds this morning."

The Squire had laid down his knife and fork, and was staring at his son in amazement, not being quick enough to guess why his son would pay him a hundred pounds.

"The truth is, sir—I'm very sorry—I was quite to blame," said Godfrey. "Fowler did pay that hundred pounds. He paid it to me, when I was over there one day last month. And Dunsey bothered me for the money, and I let him have it, because I hoped I should be able to pay it to you before this."

The Squire was purple with anger before his son had finished. "You let Dunsey have it, sir? And how long have you been so thick with Dunsey that you must conspire with him to embezzle my money? Are you turning into a scamp? I tell you I won't have it. I'll turn the whole pack of you out of the house together, and marry again. I'd have you remember, sir, my property's got no restrictions on it. Since my grandfather's time the Casses can do as they like with their land. Remember that, sir. Let Dunsey have the money! Why should you let Dunsey have the money? There's some lie at the bottom of it."

"There's no lie, sir," said Godfrey. "I wouldn't have spent the money myself, but Dunsey bothered me, and I was a fool, and let him have it. But I meant to pay it, whether he did or not. That's the whole story. I never meant to embezzle money, and I'm not the man to do it. You never knew me to be dishonest, sir."

"Where's Dunsey, then? What do you stand talking there for? Go and fetch Dunsey, as I tell you, and let him explain what he wanted the money for, and what he's done with it. He shall repent, and I'll turn him out. I said I would, and I'll do it. He shan't defy me. Go and fetch him."

"Dunsey hasn't come back, sir."

"What! Did he break his own neck, then?" said the Squire, with some disgust at the idea that he could not fulfill his threat.

"No, he wasn't hurt, I believe, for the horse was found dead, and Dunsey must have walked off. I daresay we shall see him again by-and-by.

I don't know where he is."

"And why did you let him have my money? Answer me that," said the Squire, attacking Godfrey again, since Dunsey was not within reach.

"Well, sir, I don't know," said Godfrey, hesitatingly. That was a feeble evasion, but Godfrey was not fond of lying, and, he could not think of a motive.

"You don't know? I tell you what it is, sir. You've been up to some trick, and you've been bribing him not to tell," said the Squire, with a sudden insight. Godfrey felt his heart beat violently at the nearness of his father's guess. The sudden alarm pushed him to take the next step.

"Why, sir," he said, trying to speak with careless ease, "it was a little affair between me and Dunsey. It's no matter to anybody else. It's hardly worthwhile to pry into young men's fooleries. It wouldn't have made any difference to you, sir, if I'd not had the bad luck to lose Wildfire. I should have paid you the money."

"Fooleries! Pshaw! It's time you'd finished with fooleries. And I'd have you know, sir, you must finish with 'em," said the Squire, frowning and casting an angry glance at his son. "Your goings-on are not what I shall find money for any longer. My grandfather had his stables full o' horses, and kept a good house, too, and in worse times, by what I can make out. So might I, if I hadn't four good-for-nothing fellows to hang on me like horse leeches. I've been too good a father to you all—that's what it is. But I shall change that, sir."

Godfrey was silent. He was not generally perceptive, but he had always sensed that his father's indulgence had not been out of kindness. And he had vaguely longed for some discipline that would have checked his own errant weakness and helped his better will. The Squire ate his bread and meat hastily, took a deep drink of ale, then turned his chair from the table, and began to speak again.

"It'll be all the worse for you, you know— you'll have to try and help me keep things together."

"Well, sir, I've often offered to take the management of things, but you seemed to think I wanted to push you out of your place."

"I know nothing o' your offering," said the Squire, whose memory consisted in certain strong impressions unmodified by detail. "But I know one who you seemed to be thinking o' marrying, and I didn't offer to put any obstacles in your way, as some fathers would. I'd prefer you married Lammeter's daughter as anybody. I suppose, if I'd told you no, you'd ha' kept on with it. But, for want o' contradiction, you've changed your mind. You're a shilly-shally fellow: you take after your poor mother. She never had a will of her own. A woman has no call for one, if she's got a proper man for her husband. But your wife would need one, for you hardly know your own mind enough to make both your legs walk one way. The lass hasn't said downright she won't have you, has she?"

"No," said Godfrey, feeling very hot and uncomfortable. "But I don't think she will."

"Think! Why haven't you the courage to ask her? Do you want to have her?"

"There's no other woman I want to marry," said Godfrey, evasively.

"Well, then, let me make the offer for you, if you haven't the pluck to do it yourself. Lammeter isn't likely to forbid his daughter to marry into my family, I should think. And as for the pretty lass, she wouldn't have her cousin— and there's nobody else, as I see, to stand in your way."

"I'd rather let it be, please sir, at present," said Godfrey, in alarm. "I think she's a little offended with me just now, and I should like to speak for myself. A man must manage these things for himself."

"Well, speak, then, and manage it, and see if you can't turn over a new leaf. That's what a man must do when he thinks o' marrying."

"I don't see how I can think of it at present, sir. You wouldn't like to settle me on one of the farms, I suppose, and I don't think she'd come to live in this house with all my brothers. It's a different sort of life than she's been used to."

"Not come to live in this house? Don't tell me. You ask her, that's all," said the Squire, with a short, scornful laugh.

"I'd rather let the thing be, at present, sir," said Godfrey. "I hope you won't try to hurry it by saying anything."

"I shall do what I choose," said the Squire, "and I shall let you know I'm master. Else you may leave and find an estate to drop into somewhere else. Go out and tell Winthrop not to go to Cox's, but wait for me. And tell 'em to get my horse saddled. And get that hack o' Dunsey's sold, and hand me the money, will you? He'll keep no more hacks at my expense. And if you know where he's sneaking—I daresay you do—you may tell him to spare himself the journey o' coming back home. Let him keep himself. He shan't hang on me anymore."

"I don't know where he is, sir. If I did, it isn't my place to tell him to keep away," said Godfrey, moving toward the door.

"Confound it, sir, don't stay arguing, but go and order my horse," said the Squire, taking up a pipe.

Godfrey left the room, hardly knowing whether he were more relieved by the sense that the interview was ended without having made any change in his position, or more uneasy that he had entangled himself still further in deceit. What had passed about his proposing to Nancy had raised a new alarm, since some after dinner words of his father's to Mr. Lammeter would oblige him to absolutely decline her when she seemed to be within his reach. He fled to his usual refuge, that of hoping for some unforeseen turn of fortune, some favorable chance that would save him from unpleasant consequences.

Chapter 10

Justice Malam was naturally regarded in Tarley and Raveloe as a man of great intellect, seeing that he could draw much wider conclusions without evidence than could be expected of people who were not on the Commission of the Peace. Such a man was not likely to neglect the clue of the tinderbox, and an inquiry was begun concerning a peddler, name unknown, with curly black hair and a foreign complexion, carrying a box of cutlery and jewelry, and wearing large rings in his ears. But either because inquiry was too slow to overtake him, or because the description applied to so many peddlers that inquiry did not know how to choose among them, weeks passed away without any change besides the lessening of interest in the case.

Dunstan Cass's absence was hardly noticed. He had once before had a quarrel with his father, and had gone off somewhere, to return at the end of six weeks to his usual swagger. His own family expected as much now, with the sole difference that the Squire was determined this time to throw him out. They never mentioned his absence, and when his uncle Kimble or Mr. Osgood noticed it, the story of his having killed Wildfire and offended his father did not surprise them. To connect Dunsey's disappearance with the robbery occurring on the same day did not occur to anyone, even Godfrey, who had better reason than anyone else to know what his brother was capable of. He remembered no mention of the weaver between them since the time, twelve years ago, when it was their boyish game to insult him. Besides, his imagination constantly created an alibi for Dunstan. He saw him in some friendly bar, where he had gone after leaving Wildfire, sponging on chance acquaintances, and thinking about coming home to torment his elder brother. Even if any brain in Raveloe had put the said two facts together, no one would have wanted to accuse a respected family of such a thing.

When the robbery was talked of at the Rainbow and elsewhere, in good company, the balance continued to waver between the rational explanation and the theory of an impenetrable mystery. The advocates of the tinderbox-and-peddler view considered the other side a gullible set, who, because they themselves were blind, supposed everybody else to be as well. The supporters of the mystery more than hinted that their opponents were shortsighted. But while poor Silas's loss stirred up Raveloe conversation, Silas himself was feeling devastated. To anyone who had observed him before he lost his gold, it might have seemed that so withered a life as his could hardly sustain a bruise. But in reality it had been an eager life, filled with immediate purpose that protected him from the cheerless unknown.

Now the protection was gone, and Marner's thoughts could no longer move in their old ways. The loom was there, and the weaving, and the growing pattern in the cloth. But the bright treasure in the hole under his feet was gone, and the prospect of handling and counting it was gone. His evenings held no delight. The thought of the money he would get by his current work could bring no joy, for it only reminded him of his loss. His heart was too crushed to put hope in a new beginning.

He filled up his time with grief. As he sat weaving, he every now and then moaned low, like one in pain. And all the evening, as he sat in his loneliness by his dull fire, he leaned his elbows on his knees, and clasped his head with his hands, and moaned very low—not as one who seeks to be heard.

And yet he was not utterly forgotten in his trouble. His misfortune had revealed him in a new light to his neighbors. Instead of a man who had more cunning than honest folks could come by, it was now apparent that Silas had not cunning enough to hold onto his own. He was generally spoken of as a "poor mushed creature," and his avoidance of company was now considered mere craziness.

This change to a kindlier feeling was shown in various ways. It was the season when well-to-do families give away pork and black pudding, and Silas's misfortune had put him in the minds of housekeepers like Mrs. Osgood. Mr. Crackenthorp, too, while he scolded Silas that his money had probably been taken from him because he thought too much of it and never came to church, gave him a present of pig's feet. Neighbors who had nothing material to give would greet Silas and discuss his misfortune at some length when they encountered him in the village. They would also take the trouble of calling at his cottage, getting him to repeat all the details on the very spot. Then they would try to cheer him by saying, "Well, Master Marner, you're no worse off than other poor folks, after all. And if you was to be crippled, the parish would give you allowance."

Mr. Macey came one evening expressly to let Silas know that recent events had given him a higher standing in Mr. Macey's eyes. He opened the conversation by saying, as soon as he had seated himself and adjusted his thumbs, "Come, Master Marner, why, you've no call to sit a-moaning. You're a deal better off to have lost your money, than to ha' kept it by foul means. I used to think, when you first come into these parts, that you were no better than you should be. You were much younger, but you were always a staring, white-faced creature, partly like a bald-faced calf. But there's no knowing: it isn't every strange thing that Old Harry's made—I mean, speaking o' toads and such. They're often harmless, like, and useful against vermin. And it's pretty much the same wi' you, as fur as I can see. Though as to the herbs and stuff to cure the breathing, if you brought that sort o' knowledge from distant parts, you might ha' been a bit freer with it. And if the knowledge wasn't well come by, why, you might ha' made up for it by coming to church regular. The children charmed by the Wise Woman were christened just as well as anyone. And that's reasonable, for if Old Harry wants to do a bit o' kindness for a holiday, who's got anything against it? That's my thinking, and I've been clerk o' this parish forty years. And so, Master Marner, as I was saying, my advice is that you keep up your spirits. As for thinking you're a deep one, with more inside you than will bear daylight, I'm not o' that opinion at all, and so I tell the neighbors. For, says I, you talk o' Master Marner making up a tale—why, it's nonsense, that is. It would take a shrewd man to make a tale like that, and he looked as scared as a rabbit."

During this lengthy address Silas had stayed motionless, leaning his elbows on his knees, and pressing his hands against his head. Mr. Macey, not doubting that he had been listened to, paused, in the expectation of some grateful reply, but Marner remained silent. He had a sense that the old man meant to be good-natured and neighborly. But the kindness fell on him as sunshine falls on the wretched—he had no heart to taste it.

"Come, Master Marner, have you got nothing to say to that?" said Mr. Macey at last, with slight impatience.

"Oh," said Marner, slowly, shaking his head between his hands, "I thank you—thank you—kindly."

"Aye, aye, to be sure: I thought you would," said Mr. Macey. "And my advice is—

have you got a Sunday suit?"

"No," said Marner.

"I doubted it," said Mr. Macey. "Now, let me advise you to get a Sunday suit. Tookey, he's a poor creature, but he's got my tailoring business, and he shall make a suit at a low price, and give you credit. Then you can come to church, and be a bit neighborly. Why, you've never heard me say 'Amen' since you come into these parts, and I recommend you to lose no time, for it'll be poor work when Tookey has it all to himself, for I may not stand with the choir again, come another winter." Here Mr. Macey paused, expecting some sign of emotion in his hearer, but not observing any, he went on. "And as for the money for the suit o' clothes, why, you get a matter of a pound a week at your weaving, Master Marner, and you're a young man, eh, for looking so mushed. Why, you couldn't ha' been twenty-five when you come into these parts, eh?"

Silas started a little at the change to a questioning tone, and answered mildly, "I can't rightly say—it's a long while since."

After receiving such an answer as this, it is not surprising that Mr. Macey observed, later on in the evening at the Rainbow, that Marner's head was "all of a muddle," and that he probably never knew when Sunday came round, which showed him a worse heathen than many a dog.

Another of Silas's comforters, besides Mr. Macey, came to him with a mind highly charged on the same topic. This was Mrs. Winthrop, the wheelwright's wife. The inhabitants of Raveloe were not severely regular in their churchgoing, and perhaps there was hardly a person in the parish who would not have held that to go to church every Sunday would have shown a greedy desire to stand well with Heaven, and get an undue advantage over their neighbors. At the same time, it was understood to be required for all who were not household servants, or young men, to take the sacrament at one of the great festivals. Squire Cass himself took it on Christmas day, while those who were thought "good" went to church with greater, though still with moderate, frequency.

Mrs. Winthrop was one of these: a highly moral woman, so eager for duties that she rose at half-past four. She had not the harsh temper that can be a condition of such habits, but was a very mild, patient woman, who was drawn to sad and serious events. She was the person always first thought of in Raveloe when there was illness or death in a family, when leeches were to be applied, or there was a sudden disappointment in a monthly nurse. She was a "comfortable woman"—good-looking, with her lips always slightly screwed, as if she were in a sickroom with the doctor or the clergyman present. But no one had seen her shed tears. She was simply grave and inclined to shake her head and sigh, almost imperceptibly, like a funereal mourner who is not a relation. It seemed surprising that Ben Winthrop, who loved his drink and his joke, got along so well with Dolly. But she took her husband's jokes and cheer as patiently as everything else, saying that "men would be so," and seeing the stronger sex as one of the animals that Heaven had made naturally troublesome, like bulls and turkeys.

This good wholesome woman was drawn strongly to Silas Marner, now that he was a sufferer. One Sunday afternoon she went to call on Silas, with her little boy Aaron and some small lard cakes, flat pastelike articles much loved in Raveloe. Aaron, an apple-cheeked youngster of seven, with a clean starched collar, needed all his adventurous curiosity to ward off the thought that the big-eyed weaver might hurt him. His doubts increased when, on arriving at the Stone Pits, they heard the mysterious sound of the loom.

"Ah, it is as I thought," said Mrs. Winthrop, sadly. They had to knock loudly before Silas heard them. But when he did come to the door he showed no impatience, as he would once have done, at an unexpected visit. Formerly, his heart had been as a locked casket with its treasure inside. But now the casket was empty, and the lock was broken. Left groping in darkness, with his support utterly gone, Silas sensed that if any help came to him it must come from without. He opened the door wide to admit Dolly, but without otherwise returning her greeting than by moving the armchair a few inches as a sign that she was to sit down in it. Dolly, as soon as she was seated, removed the white cloth that covered her lard cakes, and said in her gravest way, "The lard cakes turned out better than usual, and I'd like you to accept some, if you please. I don't eat such things myself, but men's stomachs are made so comical, they like variety—they do, I know, God help 'em."

Dolly sighed gently as she held out the cakes to Silas, who thanked her kindly and looked very close at them, absently, being accustomed to look so at everything he took into his hand. He was watched all the while by the wondering bright eyes of the small Aaron, who was peeping round from behind his mother's chair.

"There's letters on 'em," said Dolly. "I can't read 'em myself, and there's nobody, not Mr. Macey himself, who knows what they mean. But they've a good meaning, for they're on the pulpit cloth at church. What are they, Aaron, my dear?"

Aaron retreated completely behind the chair.

"Oh, stop that," said his mother, mildly. "Well, whatever the letters are, they've a good meaning. Ben says the stamp has been in our house ever since he was a little un, and his mother used to put it on the cakes. I've allays put it on too, for if there's any good, we've need of it i' this world."

"It's I.H.S.," said Silas, at which proof of learning Aaron peeped round the chair again.

"Well, to be sure, you can read 'em off," said Dolly. "Ben's read 'em to me many and many a time, but they slip out o' my mind again. More's the pity, for they're good letters, else they wouldn't be in the church. So I put 'em on all the loaves and all the cakes, though sometimes they won't hold, because o' the rising. I hope they'll bring good to you, Master Marner, for it's why I brought you the cakes. You see the letters have held better than usual."

Silas was as unable to interpret the letters as Dolly, but he understood her desire to give comfort in her quiet tones. He said, with more feeling than before—"Thank you—thank you kindly." But he laid down the cakes and seated himself absently, unconscious of any real good the cakes and the letters, or even Dolly's kindness, could do for him.

"Ah, if there's good anywhere, we've need of it," repeated Dolly, who did not lightly give up a serviceable phrase. She looked at Silas pityingly as she went on. "But you didn't hear the church bells this morning, Master Marner? I doubt you knew it was Sunday. Living so alone here, you lose your count, I daresay. Then, when your loom makes a noise, you can't hear the bells, especially now the frost kills the sound."

"Yes, I did; I heard 'em," said Silas, to whom Sunday bells were a mere accident of the day, and not part of its sacredness. There had been no bells in Lantern Yard.

"Dear heart!" said Dolly, pausing before she spoke again. "But what a pity it is you should work on Sunday. There's the bakehouse, if you could make up your mind to spend a twopence on the oven now and then. You might carry your bit o' dinner there, for it's right to have a bit o' something hot for Sunday, and make your dinner different from Saturday. But now, for Christmas day, if you was to take your dinner to the bakehouse, and go to church, and see the holly and the yew, and hear the anthem, and then take the sacrament, you'd be a deal better, and you'd know which end you stood on. You could put your trust i' Them that knows better than we do."

Dolly's advice, which was unusually long for her, was said in the soothing tone with which she would have tried to convince a sick man to take his medicine, or a basin of gruel for which he had no appetite. Silas had never before been closely urged to go to church, and he was too direct and simple to evade Dolly's appeal.

"Nay, nay," he said, "I know nothing o' church. I've never been to church."

"No!" said Dolly, in a low tone of wonderment. Then thinking of Silas's arrival from an unknown country, she said, "Did they have no church where you was born?"

"Oh, yes," said Silas, meditatively, sitting in his usual posture of leaning on his knees, and supporting his head. "There was churches—a many—it was a big town. But I knew nothing of 'em—I went to chapel."

Dolly was much puzzled at this new word, but she was rather afraid of inquiring further, lest "chapel" might mean some wicked place. After a little thought, she said, "Well, Master Marner, it's never too late to turn over a new leaf, and if you've never had no church, there's no telling the good it'll do you. For I feel so comfortable when I've been and heard the prayers, and the singing to the praise and glory o' God, as Mr. Macey gives out, and Mr. Crackenthorp saying good words, and especially on Sacramen' Day. If a bit o' trouble comes, I feel that I can put up wi' it, for I've looked for help i' the right place, and given myself up to Them as we must all give ourselves up."

Poor Dolly's explanation of her simple Raveloe theology fell on deaf ears, for there was no word in it that could remind Silas of what he had known as religion. He was quite baffled by the plural pronoun, which was no heresy of Dolly's, but only her way of not sounding too familiar. He remained silent, not wanting to say that he would go to church. Indeed, Silas was so unaccustomed to talk beyond the brief questions and answers necessary for the transaction of his simple business, words did not easily come to him without a distinct purpose.

But now, little Aaron, having become used to the weaver's presence, had gone to his mother's side. Silas, seeming to notice him for the first time, tried to return Dolly's good will by offering the lad a bit of lard cake. Aaron shrank back a little, and rubbed his head against his mother's shoulder, but still thought the piece of cake worth the risk of putting his hand out for it.

"Oh, for shame, Aaron," said his mother, taking him on her lap. "Why, you don't want cake again for a while. He's very healthy," she went on, with a little sigh. "He's my youngest, and we spoil him sadly, for either me or the father must always have him in our sight—that we must."

She stroked Aaron's brown head, and thought it must do Master Marner good to see such a "picture of a child." But Marner, on the other side of the hearth, saw the neat-featured rosy face as a mere dim circle, with two dark spots in it.

"And he's got a voice like a bird—you wouldn't think," Dolly went on. "He can sing a Christmas carol that his father's taught him. I take it as a sign that he'll come to good, as he can learn the good tunes so quick. Come, Aaron, stand up and sing the carol to Master Marner, come."

Aaron replied by rubbing his forehead against his mother's shoulder.

"Oh, that's naughty," said Dolly, gently. "Stan' up, when mother tells you, and let me hold the cake till you've done."

Aaron was not unwilling to display his talents, even to an ogre, under good circumstances. After a few more signs of coyness, consisting chiefly in rubbing the backs of his hands over his eyes, and then peeping between them at Master Marner, to see if he looked anxious for the carol, he at last allowed his head to be duly adjusted, and standing behind the table, so that he looked like a cherubic head untroubled with a body, he began with a clear chirp, "God rest you, merry gentlemen, Let nothing you dismay, For Jesus

Christ our Savior was born on Christmas day."

Dolly listened with a devout look, glancing at Marner in some confidence that this song would help to lure him to church.

"That's Christmas music," she said, when Aaron had ended, and had gotten his piece of cake again. "There's no music like Christmas music. At church, Master Marner, with the bassoon and the voices, you can't help thinking you've got to a better place already. I wouldn't speak ill o' this world, seeing that Them put us in it who knows best—but what wi' the drink, and the quarreling, and the bad illnesses, and the hard dying, as I've seen time and again, one's thankful to hear of a better world. The boy sings pretty, don't he, Master Marner?"

"Yes," said Silas, absently, "very pretty."

The Christmas carol, with its hammerlike rhythm, had fallen on his ears as strange music, quite unlike a hymn, and had none of the effect Dolly expected. But he wanted to show her that he was grateful, and the only way that occurred to him was to offer Aaron a bit more cake.

"Oh, no, thank you, Master Marner," said Dolly, holding down Aaron's willing hands. "We must be going home now. And so I wish you goodbye, Master Marner. If you ever feel you can't fend for yourself, I'll come and clean up for you, and get you a bit o' food. But I beg and pray of you to leave off weaving on Sunday, for it's bad for soul and body. The money that comes from it will be a bad bed to lie down on at the last, if it doesn't fly away, nobody knows where, like the white frost. And you'll excuse me being that free with you, Master Marner, for I wish you well—I do. Make your bow, Aaron."

Silas said "goodbye, and thank you kindly," as he opened the door for Dolly, but he couldn't help feeling relieved when she was gone—relieved that he might weave again and moan at his ease. Her simple view of life and its comforts, by which she had tried to cheer him, was only like a report of unknown objects, which he could not imagine. The fountains of human love and of faith in a divine love had not yet been unlocked, and his soul was still a shrunken stream. But its little groove of sand was blocked up, and it wandered in confusion.

And so, Silas spent his Christmas day in loneliness, eating his meat with a sad heart, though the meat had come to him as a neighborly present. In the morning he looked out on the black frost that seemed to press cruelly on every blade of grass, while the half-icy red pool shivered under the bitter wind. But towardsevening the snow began to fall, shutting him up with his grief. He sat in his robbed home through the livelong evening, not caring to close his shutters or lock his door, pressing his head between his hands and moaning, till the cold grasped him and told him that his fire was gray.

Nobody in this world but himself knew that he was the same Silas Marner who had once loved his fellow with tender love, and trusted in an unseen goodness. Even to himself that past experience had become dim.

But in Raveloe village the bells rang merrily, and the church was fuller than all through the rest of the year, with red faces among the abundant dark green boughs. Those green boughs, and the hymn and anthem never heard but at Christmas, brought a sense of exultation that something great and mysterious had been done for everyone in heaven above and in earth below. Then the red faces made their way through the black biting frost to their own homes, feeling themselves free for the rest of the day to eat, drink, and be merry, and using that Christian freedom without restraint.

At Squire Cass's family party that day nobody mentioned Dunstan. Indeed, nobody was sorry for his absence, or feared it would be too long. The doctor and his wife, uncle and aunt Kimble, were there, and the annual Christmas talk was carried through without any omissions, rising to the climax of Mr. Kimble's experience when he walked the London hospitals thirty years back. Then they played cards, accompanied by drinks all round.

But the party on Christmas day, being a strictly family party, was not the most brilliant celebration of the season at the Red House. It was the great dance on New Year's Eve that made the glory of Squire Cass's hospitality. This was the occasion when all the society of Raveloe and Tarley met and behaved themselves appropriately. Fair dames came in open carriages, supplied with more than their evening costume, for the feast was not to end with a single evening. The Red House was provisioned as if for a siege, and as for the spare featherbeds ready to be laid on floors, they were as plentiful as might naturally be expected in a family that had killed its own geese for many generations.

Godfrey Cass was looking forward to this New Year's Eve with a foolish reckless longing, that made him half deaf to his usual companion, Anxiety.

"Dunsey will be coming home soon. There will be a great blowup, and how will you bribe him to keep quiet?" said Anxiety.

"Oh, he won't come home before New Year's Eve, perhaps," said Godfrey. "And I shall sit by Nancy then, and dance with her, and get a kind look from her in spite of herself."

"But money is wanted in another quarter,"

said Anxiety, in a louder voice, "and how will you get it without selling your mother's diamond pin? And if you don't get it . . . ?"

"Well, but something may happen to make things easier. At any rate, there's one pleasure for me close at hand: Nancy is coming."

"Yes, and suppose your father should do something that will oblige you to decline marrying her—and to give your reasons?"

"Hold your tongue, and don't worry me. I can see Nancy's eyes, just as they will look at me, and feel her hand in mine already."

But Anxiety went on in noisy Christmas company, refusing to be utterly quieted even by much drinking.

Chapter 11

Some women would not look their best seated in an open carriage, wearing a drab beaver bonnet, with a crown resembling a small stewpot, and a garment like a miniature cape. It was all the greater triumph to Miss Nancy Lammeter's beauty that she looked thoroughly bewitching in that costume, as, seated behind her tall, erect father, she looked down at the treacherous snow-covered pools and puddles, which sent up mud splashes under the stamp of Dobbin's foot. Certainly the bloom on her cheeks was at its highest color when she arrived at the door of the Red House, and saw Mr. Godfrey Cass ready to lift her from the carriage. She wished her sister Priscilla had come up at the same time, for then Mr. Godfrey should have lifted off Priscilla first. In the meantime, she would have persuaded her father to go round to the horse block instead of alighting at the doorsteps. It was very painful, when you had made it quite clear to a young man that you were determined not to marry him, for him to continue to pay you attentions. Besides, why didn't he always show the same attentions, if he meant them sincerely? Mr. Godfrey Cass sometimes behaved as if he didn't want to speak to her, taking no notice of her for weeks and weeks, and then, all of a sudden, he was quite attentive. Moreover, it was plain he had no real love for her, else he would not let people talk of him as they did. Did he suppose that Miss Nancy Lammeter was to be won by any man, squire or no squire, who led a bad life? That was not what she had been used to see in her own father, who was the soberest and best man in the country—only a little hot and hasty now and then, if things were not done right.

All these thoughts rushed through Miss Nancy's mind in the moments between her first sight of Mr. Godfrey Cass standing at the door and her own arrival there. Happily, the Squire came out too and gave a loud greeting to her father, so that the noise concealed her confusion while she was being lifted by strong arms, which seemed to find her ridiculously small and light. She went into the house at once, since the snow was beginning to fall again, threatening the guests that were still on the road. These were a small minority, for already the afternoon was waning. There would not be too much time for the ladies who came from a distance to dress for the early tea before the dance.

There was a buzz of voices through the house, as Miss Nancy entered, mingled with the scrape of a fiddle tuning up in the kitchen. Mrs. Kimble, who did the honors at the Red House on these great occasions, came forward to meet Miss Nancy in the hall, and bring her upstairs. Mrs. Kimble was the Squire's sister, as well as the doctor's wife—a double dignity, with which her diameter was in direct proportion. A journey upstairs being rather fatiguing to her, she did not oppose Miss Nancy's request to be allowed to find her way alone to the Blue Room, where the Miss Lammeters' trunks had been put on their arrival in the morning.

There was hardly a bedroom in the house where feminine compliments were not passing and ladies were not dressing in crowded conditions. Miss Nancy, as she entered the Blue Room, had to make her little formal curtsy to a group of six. On the one hand, there were ladies no less important than the two Miss Gunns, the wine merchant's daughters from Lytherly. They were dressed in the height of fashion, with the tightest skirts and the shortest waists. They were gazed at by Miss Ladbrook (of the Old Pastures), who felt that her own skirt must be regarded as too loose by the Miss Gunns, and also that the Miss Gunns should not go quite so far for the sake of fashion.

Miss Nancy had no sooner made her curtsy than an elderly lady came forward, whose full white muslin kerchief was in daring contrast with the puffed yellow satins and top-knotted caps of her neighbors. She approached Miss Nancy with much primness, and said, with a slow, smooth voice, "Niece, I hope you are in good health."

Miss Nancy kissed her aunt's cheek dutifully, and answered, with the same sort of amiable primness, "Quite well, I thank you, aunt. I hope you are the same."

"Thank you, niece. I keep my health for the present. And how is my brother-in-law?"

These dutiful questions and answers continued until it was confirmed that the Lammeters were all as well as usual, and the Osgoods likewise, also that niece Priscilla must certainly arrive shortly. Then Nancy was formally introduced to her aunt's visitors, the Miss Gunns, as being the daughter of a mother known to their mother, though they had never been to these parts. These ladies were so taken by surprise at finding such a lovely face and figure in an out-of-the-way country place that they began to feel some curiosity about the dress she would put on when she took off her coat. Miss Nancy, whose thoughts were as careful as her manners, remarked to herself that the Miss Gunns were rather hard-featured, and that such very low dresses were worn more out of obligation than vanity, given the appearance of their shoulders. She felt convinced, as she opened her trunk, that this must be her aunt Osgood's opinion. Miss Nancy's mind resembled her aunt's to a degree that everybody said was surprising, considering the kinship was on Mr. Osgood's side. Despite the formality of their greeting, there was a devoted attachment and mutual admiration between aunt and niece. Even Miss Nancy's refusal of her cousin Gilbert Osgood (on the ground solely that he was her cousin), though it had grieved her aunt greatly, had not in the least dissuaded her from leaving Nancy several of her hereditary ornaments.

Three of the ladies quickly retired, but the Miss Gunns stayed to see the rustic beauty's toilette. And it was really a pleasure—from the first opening of the trunk, where everything smelt of lavender and rose leaves, to the clasping of the small coral necklace that fitted closely round her little white neck. Everything belonging to Miss

Nancy was of delicate purity: not a crease was where it had no business to be. The very pins on her pincushion were stuck in a pattern she was careful to keep. As for her own person, it gave the same idea of perfect neatness as the body of a little bird. It is true that her light brown hair was cropped behind like a boy's, and was dressed in front in a number of flat rings, that lay quite away from her face. But there was no style that could make Miss Nancy's cheek and neck look less than pretty. When at last she stood complete in her silver silk, her lace tucker, her coral necklace, and coral ear drops, the Miss Gunns could see nothing to criticize except her hands, which bore the traces of butter-making, cheese-crushing, and even still coarser work. But Miss Nancy was not ashamed of that, for even while she was dressing she narrated to her aunt how she and Priscilla had packed their boxes yesterday, because this morning was baking morning. Since they were leaving home, it was desirable to make a good supply of meat pies for the kitchen.

As she finished speaking, she turned to the Miss Gunns that she might not commit the rudeness of not including them in the conversation. The Miss Gunns smiled stiffly, and thought what a pity it was that these rich country people, who could afford to buy such good

clothes, should be brought up in utter ignorance and vulgarity. She actually said "mate" for
"meat," "'appen" for "perhaps," and "'orse"
for "horse," which, to young ladies living in
good Lytherly society, who habitually said 'orse,
even in domestic privacy, and only said 'appen
on the right occasions, was necessarily shocking.
Miss Nancy, indeed, had never been to any
school higher than Dame Tedman's. Her
acquaintance with literature hardly went beyond
simple rhymes. In order to balance an account,
she was obliged to count with visible shillings.
Indeed, there is hardly a servant maid in these
days who is not better informed than Miss
Nancy. Yet she had the essential attributes of a
lady—high honesty, delicate honor in her dealings, deference to others, and refined personal
habits. Moreover, she was slightly proud and
exacting, and as loyal to a baseless opinion as
towards an erring lover.

Her anxiety about sister Priscilla happily
ended with the entrance of that cheerful looking
lady herself. After the first questions and greetings, she turned to Nancy, and surveyed her from
head to foot—then wheeled her round, to make
sure that the back view was equally faultless.

"What do you think o' these gowns, aunt
Osgood?" said Priscilla, while Nancy helped her
to undress.

"Very handsome indeed, niece," said Mrs. Osgood, with a slight increase of formality. She always thought niece Priscilla too rough.

"I'm obliged to have the same as Nancy, you know, even though I'm five years older, and it makes me look yellow. She never will have anything unless I have mine just like it, because she wants us to look like sisters. And I tell her, folks will think that I fancy that I look pretty in what she looks pretty in. For I am ugly—there's no denying that. I look like my father's family. But, law! I don't mind, do you?" Priscilla here turned to the Miss Gunns, rattling too fast to notice that her talk was not appreciated. "The pretty ones are like flycatchers—they keep the men off us. I've no opinion o' the men, Miss Gunn—I don't know about you. And as for fretting and stewing about what they'll think of you from morning till night, and making your life uneasy about what they're doing when they're out o' your sight—as I tell Nancy, no woman need do that, if she's got a good father and a good home. Let her leave it to them that have no fortune, and can't help themselves. As I say, Mr. Have-your-own-way is the best husband, and the only one I'd ever promise to obey."

The delicate process of getting her narrow gown over her head without injuring her smooth curls, obliged Miss Priscilla to pause in this rapid survey of life, and Mrs. Osgood seized the opportunity of rising and saying, "Well, niece, you'll follow us. The Miss Gunns would like to go down."

"Sister," said Nancy, when they were alone, "you've offended the Miss Gunns, I'm sure."

"What have I done, child?" said Priscilla, in some alarm.

"Why, you asked them if they minded about being ugly—you're so very blunt."

"Law, did I? Well, it popped out. It's a mercy I said no more, for I'm a bad one to live with folks when they don't like the truth. But as for being ugly, look at me, child, in this silver-colored silk—I told you how it would be—I look as yellow as a daffodil. Anybody 'ud say you wanted to make a mockery of me."

"No, Priscy, don't say so. I begged and prayed of you not to let us have this silk if you'd like another better. I was willing to have your choice, you know I was," said Nancy, in anxious self-vindication.

"Nonsense, child! You know you'd set your heart on this, and for good reason, for you're the color o' cream. It 'ud be fine doings for you to dress yourself to suit my skin. What I find fault with is the idea that I must dress myself just like you. But you do as you like with me—you always did, from when first you begun to walk. If you wanted to go the field's length, the field's length you'd go. There was no whipping you, for you looked as prim and innocent as a daisy all the while."

"Priscy," said Nancy, gently, as she fastened a coral necklace, exactly like her own, round Priscilla's neck, which was very far from being like her own, "I'm always willing to admit I'm wrong, but who shouldn't dress alike if it isn't sisters? Would you have us go about looking as if we were no kin to one another—us that have got no mother and not another sister in the world? I'd rather you'd choose, and let me wear what pleases you."

"There you go again! You'd come round to the same thing if one talked to you from Saturday night till Saturday morning. It'll be fine fun to see how you'll master your husband and never raise your voice above the singing o' the kettle all the while. I like to see the men mastered!"

"Don't talk so, Priscy," said Nancy, blushing. "You know I don't mean ever to be married."

"Oh, you never mean anything!" said Priscilla, as she arranged her discarded dress, and closed her trunk. "Who shall I have to work for when Father's gone, if you are an old maid, because some folks are no better than they should be? I haven't a bit o' patience with you—sitting on a bad egg forever, as if there wasn't a fresh one in the world. One old maid's enough out o' two sisters, and I shall do credit to a single life, for God A'mighty meant me for it. Come, we can go down now. I'm as ready as a mockery can be—there's nothing more I need to frighten the crows, now I've got my ear droppers in."

As the two Miss Lammeters walked into the large parlor together, anyone who did not know the character of both might certainly have supposed that the reason the square-shouldered, clumsy, high-featured Priscilla wore a dress identical to her pretty sister's, was either the mistaken vanity of the one, or the plan of the other to set off her own rare beauty. But the good-natured cheeriness and common sense of Priscilla would soon have erased the one suspicion, and the modest calm of Nancy's speech and manners revealed a mind without such schemes.

Places of honor had been kept for the Miss Lammeters near the head of the main tea table in the parlor, now looking fresh with handsome branches of holly, yew, and laurel from the old garden. Nancy felt an inward flutter when she saw Mr. Godfrey Cass advancing to lead her to a seat between himself and Mr. Crackenthorp, while Priscilla went to the opposite side between her father and the Squire. It certainly did make some difference to Nancy that the lover she had given up was the most important young man in the parish—at home in a grand parlor, where she might one day have been mistress, as "Madam Cass," the Squire's wife. These circumstances strengthened her resolve that the most dazzling rank should not induce her to marry a man whose conduct showed him careless of his character. Yet "love once, love always," was the motto of a true and pure woman, and no man should ever make her destroy the dried flowers that she treasured, and always would treasure, for Godfrey Cass's sake. And Nancy was capable of keeping her word to herself under very trying conditions. Nothing but a becoming blush betrayed her thoughts as she accepted the seat next to Mr. Crackenthorp. She was so instinctively neat in all her actions, and her pretty lips met each other with such quiet firmness, that it would have been difficult for her to appear agitated.

The rector could not let a charming blush pass without an appropriate compliment. He was a merry-eyed, gray-haired man, wearing an ample, many-creased white neck cloth.

"Ha, Miss Nancy," he said, turning his head within his cravat and smiling down pleasantly, "when anybody pretends this has been a severe winter, I shall tell them I saw the roses blooming on New Year's Eve—eh, Godfrey, what do you say?"

Godfrey made no reply, and avoided looking at Nancy too directly. Though these compliments were held to be in excellent taste in old-fashioned Raveloe society, reverent love has a politeness of its own. But the Squire was rather impatient at Godfrey's showing himself a dull spark in this way. By this advanced hour of the day, the Squire was always in higher spirits than at the breakfast table, and enjoyed being noisily jolly and patronizing. At present, the Squire had only given an express welcome to the heads of families as they appeared. But as the evening deepened, his hospitality spread, till he had tapped the youngest guests on the back and shown a peculiar fondness for their presence, in the full belief that they must feel happy belonging to a parish where there was such a hearty man as Squire Cass to invite them and wish them well. Even in this early stage of the jovial mood, it was natural that he should wish to make up for his son's faults by speaking for him.

"Aye, aye," he began, "us old fellows may wish ourselves young tonight, when we see the mistletoe in the White Parlor. It's true, most things are gone back'ard in these last thirty years—the country's going down since the old king fell ill. But when I look at Miss Nancy here, I begin to think the lasses keep up their quality. I can't remember a sample to match her, not when I was a fine young fellow, and thought a deal about my pigtail. No offence to you, madam," he added, bending to Mrs. Crackenthorp, who sat by him. "I didn't know you when you were as young as Miss Nancy here."

Mrs. Crackenthorp was a small blinking woman, who fidgeted incessantly with her lace, ribbons, and gold chain, turning her head about and making subdued noises, very much like a guinea pig that twitches its nose. She now blinked and fidgeted towards the Squire, and said, "Oh, no—no offence."

This emphatic compliment of the Squire's to Nancy was felt by others besides Godfrey to have a diplomatic significance. Her father straightened his back, as he looked gravely across the table at her. He was not going to lose a jot of his dignity by seeming elated at the notion of a match between his family and the Squire's. He was gratified by any honor paid to his daughter, but he must see a change in several ways before giving his consent. His healthy physique and high-featured firm face, which looked as if it had never been flushed by excess, was in strong contrast, not only with the Squire, but with the Raveloe farmers generally.

"Miss Nancy's wonderful like what her mother was, though, isn't she, Kimble?" said the stout lady of that name, looking round for her husband.

But Doctor Kimble, a thin and agile man, was flitting about the room with his hands in his pockets, making himself agreeable to his feminine patients, and being welcomed everywhere as a doctor by hereditary right. Time out of mind the Raveloe doctor had been a Kimble, which was inherently a doctor's name. It was difficult to contemplate the melancholy fact that the actual Kimble had no son, so that his practice might one day be handed over to a successor with the unfitting name of Taylor or Johnson. But in that case the wiser people in Raveloe would employ Dr. Blick of Flitton.

"Did you speak to me, my dear?" said the authentic doctor, coming quickly to his wife's side. But, as if foreseeing that she would be too much out of breath to repeat her remark, he went on immediately. "Ha, Miss Priscilla, the sight of you revives the taste of that super excellent pork pie. I hope the batch isn't near an end."

"Yes, indeed, it is, doctor," said Priscilla. "But the next shall be as good. My pork pies don't turn out well by chance."

"Not as your doctoring does, eh, Kimble?

Because folks forget to take your medicine, eh?" said the Squire, who regarded medicine and doctors as many loyal churchmen regard the church and the clergy—telling a joke against them when he was in health, but impatiently eager for their aid when anything was the matter with him. He looked round with a triumphant laugh.

"Ah, she has a quick wit, my friend Priscilla has," said the doctor, ignoring the Squire. "She saves a little pepper to sprinkle over her talk— that's the reason she never puts too much into her pies. Now, my wife never has an answer at her tongue's end. But if I offend her, she's sure to torture my throat with black pepper the next day, or else give me the colic with watery greens. That's an awful tit for tat." Here the vivacious doctor made a pathetic grimace.

"Did you ever hear the like?" said Mrs. Kimble, laughing above her double chin with much good humor, aside to Mrs. Crackenthorp, who blinked and nodded, and seemed to intend a smile, which came out in small twitchings and noises.

"I suppose that's the sort of tit for tat adopted in your profession, Kimble, if you've a grudge against a patient," said the rector.

"Never do have a grudge against our patients," said Mr. Kimble, "except when they leave us. Then, you see, we haven't the chance of prescribing for 'em. Ha, Miss Nancy," he continued, suddenly skipping to Nancy's side, "you won't forget your promise? You're to save a dance for me, you know."

"Come, come, Kimble, don't you be too forward," said the Squire. "Give the young uns fair play. My son Godfrey will have a round with you if you run off with Miss Nancy. He's promised her for the first dance, I'll be bound. Eh, sir! What do you say?" he continued, throwing himself backward, and looking at Godfrey. "Haven't you asked Miss Nancy to open the dance with you?"

Godfrey, sorely uncomfortable at this insistence about Nancy, and afraid to think where it would end by the time his father had done his drinking before and after supper, saw no course open but to turn to Nancy and say, with as little awkwardness as possible, "No, I've not asked her yet, but I hope she'll consent. If somebody else hasn't been before me."

"No, I've not engaged myself," said Nancy, quietly, though blushingly.

"Then I hope you've no objections to dancing with me," said Godfrey.

"No, no objections," said Nancy, in a cold tone.

"Ah, well, you're a lucky fellow, Godfrey,"

said uncle Kimble. "But you're my godson, so I won't stand in your way. Else I'm not so very old, eh, my dear?" he went on, skipping to his wife's side again. "You wouldn't mind my having a second wife after you were gone—not if I cried a good deal first?"

"Come, come, take a cup o' tea and stop your tongue, do," said good-humored Mrs. Kimble, feeling some pride in a husband who must be regarded as so clever and amusing by the company generally. If he had only not been terrible at cards!

While familiar personalities were enlivening the tea in this way, the sound of the fiddle approaching made the young people look at each other with sympathetic impatience for the end of the meal.

"Why, there's Solomon in the hall," said the Squire, "and playing my fav'rite tune, I believe—'The Flaxen-headed Ploughboy'—he's giving us a hint that we aren't enough in a hurry to hear him play. Bob!" He called out to his third long-legged son, who was at the other end of the room. "Open the door, and tell Solomon to come in. He shall give us a tune here."

Bob obeyed, and Solomon walked in, fiddling as he walked, for he would on no account break off in the middle of a tune.

"Here, Solomon," said the Squire, with

loud patronage. "Round here, my man. Ah, I knew it was 'The Flaxen-headed Ploughboy.' There's no finer tune."

Solomon Macey, a small sturdy old man with an abundant crop of long white hair reaching nearly to his shoulders, came over, bowing reverently while he fiddled. As soon as he had repeated the tune and lowered his fiddle, he bowed again to the Squire and the rector, and said, "I hope I see your honor and your reverence well, wishing you health and long life and a happy New Year. And wishing the same to you, Mr. Lammeter, sir, and to the other gentlemen, and the madams, and the young lasses."

As Solomon uttered the last words, he bowed in all directions. Then he immediately fell into the tune that he knew would be taken as a special compliment by Mr. Lammeter.

"Thank ye, Solomon, thank ye," said Mr. Lammeter when the fiddle paused again. "That's 'Over the Hills and Far Away,' that is. My father used to say to me, whenever we heard that tune, 'Ah, lad, I come from over the hills and far away.' There's many tunes I don't make head or tail of, but that speaks to me like the blackbird's whistle. I suppose it's the name."

But Solomon was already impatient to play again, and presently broke with much spirit into "Sir Roger de Coverley," at which there was a sound of chairs pushed back, and laughing voices.

"Aye, aye, Solomon, we know what that means," said the Squire, rising. "It's time to begin the dance, eh? Lead the way, then, and we'll all follow you."

So Solomon, holding his white head on one side, and playing vigorously, marched forward at the head of the gay procession into the White Parlor, where the mistletoe bough was hung, and many candles gleamed from among the berried holly boughs, reflected in the old-fashioned oval mirrors. A quaint procession! Old Solomon, in his seedy clothes and long white locks, seemed to be luring that decent company by the magic scream of his fiddle: discreet matrons in turban-shaped caps, self-conscious fair lasses in short-waisted dresses, burly fathers in large waistcoats, and sheepish sons in very long coattails.

Already Mr. Macey and a few other privileged villagers, who were allowed to be spectators on these great occasions, were seated on benches placed for them near the door, admiring the couples who had formed themselves for the dance. The Squire led off with Mrs. Crackenthorp, joining hands with the rector and Mrs. Osgood. That was as it should be—that was what everybody had been used to. It was proper for the old and middle-aged people to dance a little before sitting down to cards, as part of their social duties.

"The Squire's pretty springy, considering his weight," said Mr. Macey, "and he stamps uncommon well. But Mr. Lammeter beats 'em all for shapes. You see he holds his head like a soldier, and he isn't so pudgy as most o' the old-ish gentlefolks—they run fat in general; and he's got a fine leg. The parson's nimble enough, but he hasn't got much of a leg. It's a bit too thick down'ard, and his knees might be a bit nearer. But he might do worse, he might do worse. Though he hasn't that grand way o' waving his hand as the Squire has."

"Talk o' nimbleness, look at Mrs. Osgood," said Ben Winthrop, who was holding his son Aaron between his knees. "She trips along with her little steps, so that nobody can see how she goes. It's like she had little wheels to her feet. She doesn't look a day older than last year. She's the finest made woman there is."

"I don't heed how the women are made," said Mr. Macey, with some contempt. "They wear neither coat nor breeches: you can't make much out o' their shapes."

"Father," said Aaron, whose feet were busy beating out the tune, "how does that big cock's-feather stick in Mrs. Crackenthorp's head? Is there a little hole for it, like in my shuttlecock?"

"Hush, lad, hush. That's the way the ladies dress theirselves, that is," said the father, adding, however, in an undertone to Mr. Macey, "It does make her look funny, though—partly like a short-necked bottle wi' a long quill in it. Hey, by jingo, there's the young Squire leading off now, wi' Miss Nancy for partners! There's a lass for you! Like a pink-and-white posy. I didn't know anybody could be so pretty. I shouldn't wonder if she's Madam Cass some day, after all, for they'd make a fine match. You can find nothing against Master Godfrey's shapes, Macey, I'll bet a penny."

Mr. Macey screwed up his mouth, leaned his head further on one side, and twirled his thumbs as his eyes followed Godfrey up the dance. At last he summed up his opinion.

"Pretty well down'ard, but a bit too round in the shoulder blades. And as for them coats he gets from the Flitton tailor, they're a poor cut to pay double money for."

"Ah, Mr. Macey, you and me are two folks," said Ben, slightly indignant at this complaining. "When I've got a pot o' good ale, I like to swallow it, and do my inside good, instead o' smelling and staring at it to see if I can find fault wi' the brewing. I should like you to pick me out a finer-limbed young fellow than Master Godfrey—one that could knock you down easier, or is more pleasant looking when he's merry."

"Tchuh!" said Mr. Macey, with increased severity, "he isn't come to his right color yet: he's partly like a slack-baked pie. And I think he's got a soft place in his head, else why should he be turned round the finger by that Dunsey who nobody's seen o' late, and let him kill that fine hunting horse? And he was always after Miss Nancy, and then it all went off again, like a smell o' hot porridge, as I may say. That wasn't my way when I went a-courting."

"Ah, but maybe Miss Nancy hung off, like, and your lass didn't," said Ben.

"I should say she didn't," said Mr. Macey, significantly. "Before I said 'sniff,' I took care to know whether she'd say 'snaff,' and pretty quick too. I wasn't a-going to open my mouth, like a dog at a fly, and snap it shut again, wi' nothing to swallow."

"Well, I think Miss Nancy's a-coming round again," said Ben, "for Master Godfrey doesn't look so downhearted tonight. And I see he's taking her away to sit down, now they're at the end o' the dance. That looks like sweethearting, that does."

The reason Godfrey and Nancy had left the dance was not so tender as Ben imagined. In the close press of couples a slight accident had happened to Nancy's dress, which, while it was short enough to show her neat ankle in front, was long enough behind to be caught under the stately stamp of the Squire's foot. This had torn certain stitches at the waist, and caused much agitation in Priscilla's mind, as well as serious concern in Nancy's. Nancy had no sooner completed her duty in the figure they were dancing than she said to Godfrey, with a deep blush, that she must go and sit down till Priscilla could come to her. The sisters had already exchanged a short whisper and an open-eyed glance full of meaning. No reason less urgent than this could have prevailed on Nancy to give Godfrey this opportunity of sitting apart with her. As for Godfrey, he was feeling so happy and oblivious under the long charm of the country dance with Nancy, that he got rather bold on the strength of her confusion, and led her straight away, without asking, into the adjoining small parlor, where the card tables were set.

"Oh no, thank you," said Nancy, coldly, as soon as she saw where he was going, "not in there. I'll wait here till Priscilla's ready to come to me. I'm sorry to bring you out of the dance and make myself troublesome."

"Why, you'll be more comfortable here by yourself," said the artful Godfrey. "I'll leave you here till your sister can come." He spoke in an indifferent tone.

That was an agreeable proposition, and just what Nancy desired. Why, then, was she a little hurt that Mr. Godfrey should make it? They entered, and she seated herself on a chair against one of the card tables, as the stiffest and most unapproachable position she could choose.

"Thank you, sir," she said immediately. "I needn't give you any more trouble. I'm sorry you've had such an unlucky partner."

"That's very ill-natured of you," said Godfrey, standing by her without any sign of intended departure, "to be sorry you've danced with me."

"Oh, no, sir, I don't mean to say what's ill-natured at all," said Nancy, looking distractingly prim and pretty. "When gentlemen have so many pleasures, one dance can matter only very little."

"You know that isn't true. You know one dance with you matters more to me than all the other pleasures in the world."

It was a long, long while since Godfrey had said anything so direct as that, and Nancy was startled. But her instinctive dignity and aversion to any show of emotion made her sit perfectly still, and only throw a little more decision into her voice, as she said, "No, indeed, Mr. Godfrey, that's not known to me, and I have very good reasons for thinking different. But if it's true, I don't wish to hear it."

"Would you never forgive me, then, Nancy—never think well of me—would you never think the present made up for the past? Not if I turned a good fellow, and gave up everything you didn't like?"

Godfrey was half conscious that this sudden opportunity of speaking to Nancy alone had driven him beside himself, but blind feeling had got the mastery of his tongue. Nancy felt much agitated by Godfrey's words, but this very pressure of emotion triggered all her power of self-command.

"I should be glad to see a good change in anybody, Mr. Godfrey," she answered, with the slightest difference of tone. "But it would be better if no change was wanted."

"You're very hardhearted, Nancy," said Godfrey, grumpily. "You might encourage me to be a better fellow. I'm very miserable—but you've no feeling."

"I think those have the least feeling who act wrong to begin with," said Nancy, sending out a little spark. Godfrey was delighted with that little spark, and would have liked to go on and make her quarrel with him. Nancy was usually so exasperatingly quiet and firm. But she was not indifferent to him yet.

The entrance of Priscilla, bustling forward and saying, "Dear heart alive, child, let us look at this gown," cut off Godfrey's hopes of a quarrel.

"I suppose I must go now," he said to Priscilla.

"It's no matter to me whether you go or stay," said that frank lady, searching for something in her pocket, with a preoccupied brow.

"Do you want me to go?" said Godfrey, looking at Nancy, who was now standing up on Priscilla's order.

"As you like," said Nancy, trying to recover all her former coldness, and looking down carefully at the hem of her gown.

"Then I like to stay," said Godfrey, with a reckless determination to get as much of this joy as he could tonight, and think nothing of tomorrow.

Chapter 12

While Godfrey Cass was taking sips of forgetfulness from the sweet presence of Nancy, willingly losing all memory of his hidden bond, which otherwise made him irritated with the very sunshine, Godfrey's wife was walking through the snow-covered Raveloe lanes, carrying her child in her arms.

She had intended this act of vengeance ever since Godfrey, in a fit of passion, had told her he would sooner die than acknowledge her as his wife. There would be a great party at the Red House on New Year's Eve, she knew. Her husband would be smiling and smiled upon, hiding her existence in the darkest corner of his heart. But she would ruin his pleasure: she would go in her dingy rags, with her faded face, once as handsome as the best, with her little child that had its father's hair and eyes, and reveal herself to the Squire as his eldest son's wife. Molly knew that the cause of her dingy rags was not her husband's neglect, but the demon Opium to whom she was enslaved, body and soul, except for the lingering tenderness for her hungry child. She knew this well, and yet, in sober moments, her degradation turned into bitterness towards Godfrey. He was well-off, and if she had her rights she would be well-off too. The belief that he repented his marriage, and suffered from it, only aggravated her spite.

She had set out at an early hour, but had lingered on the road, believing that if she waited under a warm shed the snow would cease to fall. She had waited longer than she knew, and now her spirit was failing in the snowy lanes. It was seven o'clock, and by this time she was not very far from Raveloe, but she did not know the way well enough to know she was near her journey's end.

She needed comfort, and she knew only one comforter—the familiar demon in her bosom. But she hesitated a moment, after drawing out the black remnant, before she raised it to her lips. In that moment the mother's love pleaded against oblivion—pleaded to be left in aching weariness, rather than to have the encircling arms benumbed so that they could not feel the dear burden. In another moment Molly had flung something away, but it was not the black remnant—it was an empty vial. And she walked on again under the breaking cloud, in a freezing wind. But she walked always more and more drowsily, and clutched more and more automatically the sleeping child at her bosom.

Slowly the demon was working his will, and cold and weariness were his helpers. Soon she felt nothing but a supreme longing to lie down and sleep. She had arrived at a spot where her footsteps were no longer checked by a hedgerow, and she had wandered vaguely, unable to distinguish any objects. She sank down against a straggling furze bush, an easy pillow enough, and the bed of snow was soft. She did not feel that the bed was cold, and did not heed whether the child would wake and cry for her. But her arms had not yet relaxed their hold, and the little one slumbered on as gently as if it had been rocked in a lace-trimmed cradle.

But the complete numbness came at last: the fingers lost their tension, the arms unbent. Then the little head fell away from the bosom, and the blue eyes opened wide on the cold starlight. At first there was a little cry of "mammy," and an effort to get back the pillowing arm and bosom. But mammy's ear was deaf, and the pillow slipped away backward.

Suddenly, as the child rolled down on its mother's knees, all wet with snow, it saw a bright glancing light on the white ground. It was immediately absorbed in watching the bright living thing running toward it, yet never arriving. In an instant the child had slipped on all fours, and held out one little hand to catch the gleam. But the gleam would not be caught in that way, and now the head came up to see where the cunning gleam came from. It came from a very bright place. The little one, rising on its legs, toddled through the snow, the old grimy shawl in which it was wrapped trailing behind it, and the queer little bonnet dangling at its back. It toddled to the open door of Silas Marner's cottage, and right up to the warm hearth, where there was a bright fire of logs and sticks, which had thoroughly warmed Silas's greatcoat spread out on the bricks to dry. The little one, used to being left by itself for long hours without notice from its mother, squatted down on the coat, and spread its tiny hands toward the blaze, in perfect contentment, gurgling and babbling at the cheerful fire, like a new-hatched gosling beginning to find itself comfortable. But soon the warmth had a lulling effect, and the little golden head sank down on the old sack, and the eyes closed.

But where was Silas Marner while this

strange visitor had come to his hearth? He was in the cottage, but he did not see the child. During the last few weeks, since he had lost his money, he had developed the habit of opening his door and looking out from time to time, as if he thought that his money might be somehow coming back to him, or that some trace, some news of it, might be mysteriously on the road. It was chiefly at night, when he was not occupied in his loom, that he did this. In the evening twilight, and later whenever the night was not dark, Silas looked out on that narrow area round the Stone Pits, listening and gazing with yearning.

This morning he had been told by some of his neighbors that it was New Year's Eve. He must sit up and hear the old year rung out and the new rung in, because that was good luck, and might bring his money back again. This was only a friendly Raveloe way of joking with the half-crazy oddities of a miser, but it had thrown Silas into a more than usually excited state. Since the start of twilight he had opened his door again and again, only to shut it immediately at seeing everything hidden by the falling snow. But the last time he opened it the snow had stopped, and the clouds were parting here and there. He stood and listened, and gazed for a long while. There was something on the road coming toward him then, but he caught no sign of it. The stillness and the wide trackless snow seemed to intensify his solitude, and give it the chill of despair. He went in again, and put his right hand on the latch of the door to close it. But he was frozen by the invisible wand of catalepsy, and stood like a statue, with wide but sightless eyes, holding open his door, powerless to resist either the good or the evil that might enter.

When Marner returned to his senses, he closed his door, unaware of any change, except that the light had grown dim, and that he was chilled and faint. He thought he had been too long standing at the door and looking out. Turning toward the hearth, he seated himself on his fireside chair, and was stooping to push the logs together, when, to his blurred vision, it seemed as if there were gold on the floor in front of the hearth. Gold! His own gold brought back to him as mysteriously as it had been taken away! He felt his heart begin to beat violently, and for a few moments he was unable to stretch out his hand and grasp the restored treasure.

The heap of gold seemed to glow and get larger beneath his agitated gaze. He leaned forward at last, and stretched forth his hand, but instead of the hard coin, his fingers encountered soft warm curls. In utter amazement, Silas fell on his knees and bent his head low to examine the marvel: it was a sleeping child—a round, fair thing, with soft yellow rings all over its head. Could this be his little sister come back to him in a dream—his little sister whom he had carried about in his arms for a year before she died, when he was a small boy without shoes or stockings? Was it a dream?

He rose to his feet again, pushed his logs together, and, throwing on some dried leaves and sticks, raised a flame. But the flame did not erase the vision—it only lit up more distinctly the little round form of the child, and its shabby clothing. It was very much like his little sister. Silas sank into his chair powerless, under the double presence of an inexplicable surprise and a rush of memories. How and when had the child come in without his knowledge? But along with that question, there was a vision of the old home and the old streets leading to Lantern Yard. And within that vision another, of the thoughts he had had in those places. The thoughts were strange to him now, like old friendships impossible to revive. Yet he had a dreamy feeling that this child was somehow a message from that far-off life, stirring old sensations of tenderness, and awe of a higher power.

But there was a cry on the hearth. The child had awakened, and Marner stooped to lift her on his knee. She clung round his neck, and burst louder and louder into cries of "mammy." Silas pressed her to him, and almost unconsciously uttered sounds of hushing tenderness. He thought that some of his porridge, which had cooled by the dying fire, would do for the child if it were only warmed up a little.

He had plenty to do through the next hour. The porridge, sweetened with some dry brown sugar, stopped the cries of the little one, and made her gaze at Silas with her blue eyes as he put the spoon into her mouth. Soon she slipped from his knee and began to toddle about, but with a stagger that made Silas jump up and follow her lest she should fall against anything that would hurt her. But she only fell in a sitting posture on the ground, and began to pull at her boots, looking up at him with a crying face as if the boots hurt her.

He took her on his knee again, but it was some time before it occurred to Silas's dull bachelor mind that the wet boots were the problem, pressing on her warm ankles. He got them off with difficulty, and the baby was at once happily occupied with the mystery of her own toes, inviting Silas, with much chuckling, to consider the mystery too. But the wet boots had suggested to Silas that the child had been walking on the snow, and this awakened him to the ordinary way by which she could have entered or been brought into his house. With this new idea, he raised the child in his arms, and went to the door. As soon as he had opened it, there was the cry of "mammy" again, which Silas had not heard since the child's first hungry waking. Bending forward, he could just make out the tracks of the little feet on the virgin snow, and he followed them to the furze bushes. "Mammy!" the little one cried again and again. There was a human body, with the head sunk low in the furze, and half-covered with the shaken snow.

Chapter 13

It was after the early supper at the Red House, and the entertainment was in that stage when bashfulness had turned into easy jollity, when gentlemen could be convinced to dance a hornpipe, and when the Squire talked loudly and patted his visitors' backs. At this stage of the evening, it was usual for the servants to get their share of amusement by coming to look at the dancing, leaving the back regions of the house in solitude.

There were two doors by which the White Parlor was entered from the hall, and they were both standing open for the sake of air. The lower one was crowded with the servants and villagers, while the upper doorway was left free. Bob Cass was dancing a hornpipe, and his father, very proud of this lithe son, whom he repeatedly declared to be just like himself in his young days, was the center of a group not far from the upper door. Godfrey was standing a little way off, not to admire his brother's dancing, but to keep sight of Nancy, who was seated in the group, near her father. He stood aloof, because he wished to avoid being the subject for the Squire's fatherly jokes in connection with matrimony and Miss Nancy Lammeter's beauty. But he had the prospect of dancing with her again when the hornpipe was concluded, and meanwhile it was very pleasant to get long glances at her quite unobserved.

But when Godfrey was lifting his eyes from one of those long glances, they encountered an object as startling to him at that moment as if it had been an apparition from the dead. It was his own child, carried in Silas Marner's arms. That was his instant impression, though he had not seen the child for months. When the hope was rising that he might possibly be mistaken, Mr. Crackenthorp and Mr. Lammeter had already approached Silas. Godfrey joined them immediately, unable to rest without hearing every word. He tried to control himself, but he knew that if anyone noticed him, they would see that he was white-lipped and trembling.

But now all eyes at that end of the room were on Silas Marner. The Squire himself had risen, and asked angrily, "How's this?—what's this?—why do you come in here in this way?"

"I've come for the doctor," Silas had said, in the first moment, to Mr. Crackenthorp.

"Why, what's the matter, Marner?" said the rector. "The doctor's here. Say quietly what you want him for."

"It's a woman," said Silas, speaking low, and half-breathlessly, just as Godfrey came up. "She's dead, I think—dead in the snow at the Stone Pits—not far from my door."

Godfrey felt a great throb. There was one terror in his mind at that moment: it was that the woman might not be dead.

"Hush, hush!" said Mr. Crackenthorp. "Go out into the hall there. I'll fetch the doctor to you. Found a woman in the snow, and thinks she's dead," he added, speaking low to the Squire. "Better say as little about it as possible: it will shock the ladies. Just tell them a poor woman is ill from cold and hunger. I'll go and fetch Kimble."

By this time, however, the ladies had pressed forward, curious to know what could have brought the solitary linen weaver there under such strange circumstances. And they were interested in the pretty child, who, half alarmed and half attracted by the brightness and the numerous company, now frowned and hid her face, then lifted up her head again and looked round, until a touch or a coaxing word brought back the frown, and made her bury her face with new determination.

"What child is it?" said several ladies at once, and, among the rest, Nancy Lammeter, addressing Godfrey.

"I don't know—some poor woman's who has been found in the snow, I believe," was the answer Godfrey wrung from himself with a terrible effort.

"Why, you'd better leave the child here, then, Master Marner," said good-natured Mrs. Kimble, hesitating, however, to take those dingy clothes into contact with her own ornamented satin bodice. "I'll tell one o' the girls to fetch it."

"No—no—I can't part with her, I can't let her go," said Silas, abruptly. "She's come to me—I've a right to keep her."

The idea of taking the child from him had come to Silas quite unexpectedly, and his speech was impulsive. A minute before, he had no clear intention about the child.

"Did you ever hear the like?" said Mrs. Kimble, in mild surprise, to her neighbor.

"Now, ladies, I must trouble you to stand aside," said Mr. Kimble, coming from the card room, in some bitterness at the interruption, but drilled by the long habit of his profession into obedience to unpleasant calls, even when he was hardly sober.

"It's a nasty business turning out now, eh, Kimble?" said the Squire. "He might ha' gone for your young fellow—the apprentice, there— what's his name?"

"Might? Aye—what's the use of talking about might?" growled uncle Kimble, hastening out with Marner, and followed by Mr. Crackenthorp and Godfrey. "Get me a pair of thick boots, Godfrey, will you? And have somebody run to Winthrop's and fetch Dolly—she's the best woman to get. Ben was here himself before supper. Is he gone?"

"Yes, sir, I met him," said Marner. "But I couldn't stop to tell him anything, only I said I was going for the doctor, and he said the doctor was at the Squire's."

The child, no longer distracted by the bright light and the smiling women's faces, began to cry and call for "mammy," though always clinging to Marner, who had apparently won her confidence. Godfrey had come back with the boots, and felt the cry as if some string were drawn tight within him.

"I'll go," he said, hastily, eager for some movement. "I'll go and fetch the woman—Mrs. Winthrop."

"Oh, pooh—send somebody else," said

uncle Kimble, hurrying away with Marner.

Godfrey, too, had disappeared to get his hat and coat, realizing that he must not look like a madman. But he rushed out of the house into the snow without heeding his thin shoes.

In a few minutes he was on his rapid way to the Stone Pits by the side of Dolly, who was much concerned at a young gentleman's getting his feet wet.

"You'd better go back, sir," said Dolly, with respectful compassion. "You've no call to catch cold. I'd ask you if you'd be so good as tell my husband to come, on your way back—he's at the Rainbow, I'm sure."

"No, I'll stay, now I'm out—I'll stay outside here," said Godfrey, when they came opposite Marner's cottage. "You can come and tell me if I can do anything."

"Well, sir, you're very good. You've a tender heart," said Dolly, going to the door.

Godfrey was too painfully preoccupied to feel a twinge of embarrassment at this undeserved praise. He walked up and down, unconscious that he was plunging ankle-deep in snow, unconscious of everything but trembling suspense about what was going on in the cottage. No, not quite unconscious of everything else. Deeper down, and half-smothered by passionate desire and dread, there was the sense that he ought to accept the consequences of his deeds, own up to the miserable wife, and claim the helpless child. But he had not moral courage enough to do so, and his mind leaped toward the sudden prospect of release from his long bondage.

"Is she dead?" he asked himself. "If she is, I may marry Nancy. Then I shall be a good fellow in future, and have no secrets, and the child shall be taken care of somehow." But across that vision came the other possibility: "She may live, and then it's all up with me."

Godfrey never knew how long it was before the door of the cottage opened and Mr. Kimble came out. He went forward to meet his uncle, prepared to suppress the agitation he must feel, whatever news he was to hear.

"I waited for you, as I'd come so far," he said, speaking first.

"Pooh, it was nonsense for you to come out. Why didn't you send one of the men? There's nothing to be done. She's dead—has been dead for hours, I should say."

"What sort of woman is she?" said Godfrey, feeling the blood rush to his face.

"A young woman, but emaciated, with long black hair. Some vagrant, quite in rags. She's got a wedding ring on, however. They must fetch her away to the workhouse tomorrow. Come, come along."

"I want to look at her," said Godfrey. "I think I saw such a woman yesterday. I'll overtake you in a minute or two."

Mr. Kimble went on, and Godfrey turned back to the cottage. He cast only one glance at the dead face on the pillow, which Dolly had smoothed with decent care. He remembered that last look at his unhappy hated wife so well, that every line in the worn face was present to him when he would tell the full story of this night sixteen years later.

He turned immediately toward the hearth, where Silas Marner sat lulling the child. She was perfectly quiet now, but not asleep, soothed by sweet porridge and warmth into a wide-gazing calm. The wide-open blue eyes looked up at Godfrey's without any uneasiness or sign of recognition. The child could make no claim on its father, and the father felt a strange conflict of regret and joy when the blue eyes turned away from him slowly, and fixed themselves on the weaver's queer face, which was bent low down to look at them.

"You'll take the child to the parish tomorrow?" asked Godfrey, speaking as indifferently as he could.

"Who says so?" said Marner, sharply. "Will they make me take her?"

"Why, you wouldn't like to keep her, should

you—an old bachelor like you?"

"Till anybody shows they've a right to take her away from me," said Marner. "The mother's dead, and I reckon she's got no father. She's a lone thing, and I'm a lone thing. My money's gone, I don't know where—and she is come from I don't know where. I know nothing—I'm partly amazed."

"Poor little thing!" said Godfrey. "Let me give something toward finding her clothes."

He put his hand in his pocket and found half-a-guinea, and, after thrusting it into Silas's hand, he hurried out of the cottage to overtake Mr. Kimble.

"Ah, I see it's not the same woman I saw," he said, as he came up. "It's a pretty little child. The old fellow seems to want to keep it, which is strange for a miser like him. But I gave him a trifle to help him out. The parish isn't likely to quarrel with him for the right to keep the child."

"No, but I've seen the time when I might have quarreled with him for her myself. It's too late now, though. If the child ran into the fire, your aunt's too fat to overtake it. She could only sit and grunt like an alarmed pig. But what a fool you are, Godfrey, to come out in your dancing shoes and stockings in this way. What do you mean by such foolishness, young fellow?

Has Miss Nancy been cruel, and do you want to spite her by spoiling your shoes?"

"Oh, everything has been disagreeable tonight. I was tired to death of jigging and gallanting, and that bother about the hornpipes. And I'd got to dance with the other Miss Gunn," said Godfrey, glad of the deception his uncle had suggested to him.

He reappeared in the White Parlor with dry feet, and with a sense of relief and gladness that was too strong for painful thoughts to struggle with. For could he not venture now, whenever opportunity offered, to say tender things to Nancy Lammeter—to promise her and himself that he would always be just what she would desire? There was no danger that his dead wife would be recognized, for those were not days of active inquiry and wide report. As for the registry of their marriage, that was a long way off, buried in unturned pages, away from everyone's interest but his own. Dunsey might betray him if he came back, but he might be won to silence.

And when events turn out so much better for a man than he has had reason to expect, is it not proof that his conduct has been less foolish than it might otherwise have appeared? Where, after all, would be the use of his confessing the past to Nancy Lammeter, and throwing away his happiness and hers? He felt some confidence that she loved him. As for the child, he would see that she was cared for: he would do everything but own her. Perhaps she would be just as happy in life without being owned by her father. At least, the father would be much happier without owning the child.

Chapter 14

There was a pauper's burial that week in Raveloe, and at Kench Yard in Batherley it was known that the dark-haired woman with the fair child, who had lately come to lodge there, was gone away again. That was the only notice taken that Molly had disappeared from the eyes of men. But the unwept death, which, to the general lot, seemed as trivial as the summer-shed leaf, acted with the force of destiny on certain human lives, shaping their joys and sorrows even to the end.

Silas Marner's determination to keep the "tramp's child" was matter of hardly less surprise and gossip in the village than the robbery of his money. That softening of feeling toward him which dated from his misfortune, that merging of suspicion and dislike in a rather contemptuous pity for him as lone and crazy, was now accompanied with a more active sympathy, especially amongst the women. Notable mothers and lazy ones alike were interested in how a lone man would manage with a two-year-old child on his hands, and were equally ready with their suggestions: the notable chiefly telling him what he had better do, and the lazy ones being emphatic in telling him what he would never be able to do.

Among the notable mothers, Dolly Winthrop was the one whose neighborly advice was the most acceptable to Marner, for it was given without any show of bustling instruction. Silas had shown her the half-guinea given to him by Godfrey, and had asked her what he should do about getting some clothes for the child.

"Eh, Master Marner," said Dolly, "there's no call to buy no more than a pair o' shoes. I've got the little petticoats that Aaron wore five years ago, and it's ill spending the money on them baby clothes, for the child will grow like grass i' May, bless it—that she will."

And the same day Dolly brought her bundle, and displayed to Marner, one by one, the tiny garments, most of them patched and darned, but clean and neat as fresh sprung herbs. This was the introduction to a great ceremony with soap and water, from which Baby came out in new beauty, and sat on Dolly's knee, handling her toes and chuckling and patting her palms together with an air of having made several discoveries about herself, which she communicated by alternate sounds of "gug-gug-gug," and "mammy." The "mammy" was not a cry of need or uneasiness, for she had been used to saying it without receiving anything in return.

"The angels in heaven couldn't be prettier," said Dolly, rubbing the golden curls and kissing them. "And to think of her being covered wi' them dirty rags—and the poor mother—froze to death. But Them took care of it, and brought her to your door, Master Marner. The door was open, and she walked in over the snow, as if she had been a little starved robin. Didn't you say the door was open?"

"Yes," said Silas, meditatively. "Yes—the door was open. The money's gone I don't know where, and she came from I don't know where."

He had not mentioned to anyone his unconsciousness of the child's entrance, shrinking from questions which might lead to the fact he himself suspected—namely, that he had been in one of his trances.

"Ah," said Dolly, "it's like the night and the morning, and the sleeping and the waking, and the rain and the harvest—one goes and the other comes, and we know not how nor where. We may strive and scratch, but it's little we can do after all. The big things come and go wi' no striving o' our own—they do, that they do. I think you're in the right to keep the little one, Master Marner, seeing as she's been sent to you, though there's folks who thinks different. You'll be a bit bothered with her while she's so little. But I'll come, and see to her for you. I've a bit o' time to spare most days, for when one gets up i' the morning, the clock seems to stan' still toward ten, afore it's time to go about the cooking. So, as I say, I'll come and see to the child for you."

"Thank you . . . kindly," said Silas, hesitating a little. "I'll be glad if you'll tell me things. But," he added, uneasily, leaning forward to look at Baby with some jealousy, as she was resting her head backward against Dolly's arm, and eyeing him contentedly from a distance, "But I want to do things for her myself, else she may get fond o' somebody else, and not fond o' me. I've been used to fending for myself in the house—I can learn, I can learn."

"Eh, to be sure," said Dolly, gently. "I've seen men as are wonderful handy wi' children. The men are awkward mostly, God help 'em— but when the drink's out of 'em, they aren't unsensible, though they're bad for leeching and bandaging—so fiery and unpatient. You see this goes first, next to the skin," proceeded Dolly, taking up the little shirt, and putting it on.

"Yes," said Marner, docilely, bringing his eyes very close, that they might be initiated in the mysteries, whereupon Baby seized his head with both her small arms, and put her lips against his face with purring noises.

"See there," said Dolly, with a woman's tender tact, "she's fondest o' you. She wants to go o' your lap, I'll be bound. Go, then. Take her, Master Marner. You can put the things on, and then you can say that you've done for her from the first of her coming to you."

Marner took her on his lap, trembling with an emotion mysterious to himself, at something unknown dawning on his life. Thought and feeling were so confused within him, that if he had tried to give them utterance, he could only have said that the child had come instead of the gold—that the gold had turned into the child. He took the garments from Dolly, and put them on under her teaching, interrupted, of course, by Baby's gymnastics.

"There, then! Why, you take to it quite easy, Master Marner," said Dolly. "But what shall you do when you're forced to sit in your loom? For she'll get busier and more mischievous every day—she will, bless her. It's lucky you've got that high hearth instead of a grate, for that keeps the fire more out of her reach. But if you've got anything as can be spilt or broke, or that could cut her fingers off, she'll be at it."

Silas meditated a little while. "I'll tie her to the leg o' the loom," he said at last. "Tie her with a good long strip o' something."

"Well, mayhap that'll do, as it's a little girl, for they're easier persuaded to sit i' one place than the lads. I know what the lads are, for I've had four, and if you was to tie 'em up, they'd make a fighting and a crying like you was ringing the pigs. But I'll bring you my little chair, and some bits o' red rag and things for her to play with. She'll sit and chatter to 'em as if they was alive. Eh, if it wasn't a sin to the lads to wish 'em made different, bless 'em, I should ha' been glad for one of 'em to be a little girl. I could ha' taught her to scour, and mend, and the knitting, and everything. But I can teach 'em this little un, Master Marner, when she gets old enough."

"But she'll be my little un," said Marner, rather hastily. "She'll be nobody else's."

"No, to be sure. You'll have a right to her, if you're a father to her, and bring her up according. But," added Dolly, coming to a point which she had determined beforehand to touch upon, "you must bring her up like christened folks's children, and take her to church, and let her learn her catechism, as my little Aaron can say off—the "I believe," and everything, and "hurt nobody by word or deed,"—as well as if he was the clerk. That's what you must do, Master Marner, if you'd do the right thing by the orphan child."

Marner's pale face flushed suddenly under a new anxiety. His mind was too busy trying to understand Dolly's words for him to think of answering her.

"And it's my belief," she went on, "that the poor little creature has never been christened, and it's only right that the parson should be spoken to. If you was willing, I'd talk to Mr. Macey about it this very day. If the child ever went anyways wrong, and you hadn't done your part by it, Master Marner, it would be a thorn i' your bed forever. I can't think it would be easy for anybody when they'd got to another world, if they hadn't done their part by the helpless children."

Dolly herself was disposed to be silent for some time now, for she had spoken from the depths of her own simple belief, and was much concerned to know whether her words would produce the desired effect on Silas. He was puzzled and anxious, for Dolly's word "christened" conveyed no distinct meaning to him. He had only heard of baptism, and had only seen the baptism of grownup men and women.

"What do you mean by 'christened'?" he said at last, timidly. "Won't folks be good to her without it?"

"Dear, dear! Master Marner," said Dolly, with gentle distress and compassion. "Had you never no father nor mother who taught you to say your prayers, and that there's good words and good things to keep us from harm?"

"Yes," said Silas, in a low voice. "I know a deal about that—used to, used to. But your ways are different: my country was a good way off." He paused a few moments, and then added, more decidedly, "But I want to do everything that can be done for the child. And whatever's right for it i' this country, and you think will do it good, I'll act according, if you'll tell me."

"Well, then, Master Marner," said Dolly, inwardly rejoiced, "I'll ask Mr. Macey to speak to the parson about it. You must fix on a name for her, because she must have a name when she's christened."

"My mother's name was Hephzibah," said Silas, "and my little sister was named after her."

"Eh, that's a hard name," said Dolly. "I partly think it isn't a christened name."

"It's a Bible name," said Silas, old ideas recurring.

"Then I've no call to speak again' it," said Dolly, rather startled by Silas's knowledge. "You see I'm no scholar, and I'm slow at catching the words. But it was awkward calling your little sister by such a hard name, when you'd got nothing big to say, wasn't it, Master Marner?"

"We called her Eppie," said Silas.

"Well, if it was not wrong to shorten the name, it would be a deal handier. And so I'll go now, Master Marner, and I'll speak about the christening afore dark. I wish you the best o' luck, and it's my belief as it'll come to you, if you do what's right by the orphan child. And there's the inoculation to be seen to. And as to washing her bits o' things, you need look to nobody but me, for I can do 'em with one hand when I've got my suds about. Eh, the blessed angel! You'll let me bring my Aaron one o' these days, and he'll show her his little cart that his father's made for him, and the black-and-white pup he's rearing."

Baby was christened, and on this occasion Silas, making himself as clean and tidy as he could, appeared for the first time within the church, and shared in the observances held sacred by his neighbors. He was quite unable, by means of anything he heard or saw, to identify the Raveloe religion with his old faith. He had no distinct idea about the baptism and the churchgoing, except that Dolly had said it was for the good of the child. In this way, as the weeks grew to months, the child created fresh links between his life and the lives from which he had shrunk. Unlike the gold, which needed nothing, and must be worshipped in close-locked solitude—which was hidden away from the daylight, was deaf to the song of birds, and started to no human tones—Eppie was a creature of endless claims and ever-growing desires, seeking and loving sunshine, and living sounds, and living movements. She made much of everything, with trust in new joy, and stirring the human kindness in all eyes that looked on her. The gold had kept his thoughts in an ever-repeated circle, leading to nothing beyond itself. But Eppie forced his thoughts onward, and carried them away to the new things that would come with the coming years, when Eppie would have learned to understand how her father Silas cared for her. The gold had asked that he should sit weaving longer and longer, deafened and blinded more and more to all things except the monotony of his loom. But Eppie called him away from his weaving, and made him think all its pauses a holiday, reawakening his senses with her fresh life, and warming him into joy because she had joy.

When the sunshine grew strong and lasting,

so that the buttercups were thick in the meadows, Silas might be seen in the sunny midday, or in the late afternoon when the shadows were lengthening under the hedgerows, strolling out with Eppie beyond the Stone Pits to where the flowers grew. They reached some favorite bank where he could sit down, while Eppie toddled to pluck the flowers, and make remarks to the winged things that murmured happily above the bright petals, calling "Dad-dad's" attention continually by bringing him the flowers. Then she would turn her ear to some sudden bird note, and Silas learned to please her by making signs of hushed stillness, that they might listen for the note to come again. When it came, she sat up and laughed with gurgling triumph. Sitting on the banks in this way, Silas began to look for the once familiar herbs again. As the leaves, with their unchanged outline and markings, lay on his palm, there was a flood of memories from which he turned away timidly, taking refuge in Eppie's little world.

As the child's mind was growing into knowledge, his mind was growing into memory. As her life unfolded, his soul, long stupefied in a cold narrow prison, was unfolding too, and returning gradually to full consciousness.

It was an influence which gathered force with every new year. The tones that stirred

Silas's heart grew distinct, and called for more distinct answers. Shapes and sounds grew clearer for Eppie's eyes and ears, and there was more that "Dad-dad" was required to notice and account for. Also, by the time Eppie was three years old, she developed a fine capacity for mischief, which exercised not only Silas's patience, but his watchfulness. Dolly Winthrop told him that punishment was good for Eppie, and that, as for rearing a child without making it tingle a little in soft and safe places now and then, it was not to be done.

"To be sure, there's another thing you might do, Master Marner," added Dolly, meditatively. "You might shut her up once in the coal hole. That was what I did wi' Aaron, for I was so silly wi' the youngest lad that I could never bear to smack him. Not that I could find i' my heart to let him stay i' the coal hole more than a minute, but it was enough to dirty him all over, so as he must be washed and dressed, and it was as good as a rod to him—that was. But I leave it to you, Master Marner, as one of 'em you must choose—either smacking or the coal hole—else she'll get so masterful, there'll be no holding her."

Silas was impressed with the melancholy truth of this last remark. But his force of mind failed before the only two penal methods open to him, not only because it was painful to hurt Eppie, but because he feared a moment's conflict with her, lest she should love him the less for it. Let even an affectionate Goliath get himself tied to a small tender thing, dreading to hurt it by pulling, and dreading still more to snap the cord, and which of the two, pray, will be master? It was clear that Eppie, with her short toddling steps, must lead father Silas a pretty dance on any fine morning when she was up to mischief.

For example, he had wisely chosen a broad strip of linen as a means of fastening her to his loom when he was busy. It made a broad belt round her waist, and was long enough to allow her to reach the bed and sit down on it, but not long enough for her to attempt any dangerous climbing.

One bright summer's morning Silas had been more engrossed than usual in setting up a new piece of work, and using his scissors in the process. These scissors, on a warning of Dolly's, had been kept carefully out of Eppie's reach. But the click of them had had a peculiar attraction for her ear, and watching the results of that click, she had learned how they worked. Silas had seated himself in his loom, and the noise of weaving had begun. But he had left his scissors on a ledge that Eppie's arm was long enough to reach. Now, like a small mouse, watching her opportunity, she stole quietly from her corner, secured the scissors, and toddled to the bed again. She had a distinct intention as to the use of the scissors, and having cut the linen strip, in two moments she had run out the open door where the sunshine was inviting her, while poor Silas believed her to be a better child than usual. It was not until he happened to need his scissors that the terrible fact burst upon him: Eppie had run out by herself—had perhaps fallen into the Stone Pit. Silas, shaken by the worst fear that could have befallen him, rushed out, calling "Eppie!" and ran eagerly about the unenclosed space, exploring the dry cavities into which she might have fallen, and then gazing with questioning dread at the smooth red surface of the water. Cold drops stood on his brow. How long had she been out? There was one hope, that she had crept through the stile and got into the fields, where he habitually took her to stroll. But the grass was high in the meadow, and there was no finding her, if she were there, except by trespassing on Mr. Osgood's crop. Still, that misdemeanor must be committed.

Poor Silas, after peering all round the hedgerows, traversed the grass, beginning to see Eppie behind every group of red sorrel, and to see her moving always farther off as he approached. The meadow was searched in vain. He got over the stile into the next field, looking with dying hope toward a small pond, which was now reduced to summer mud. Here sat Eppie, discoursing cheerfully to her own small boot, which she was using as a bucket to convey the water into a deep hoof mark, while her little naked foot was planted comfortably on a cushion of olive green mud. A redheaded calf was observing her with alarmed doubt through the opposite hedge.

Here was clearly a case of bad behavior that demanded severe treatment. But Silas, overcome with convulsive joy at finding his treasure again, could do nothing but snatch her up, and cover her with half-sobbing kisses. It was not until he had carried her home, and had begun to think of the necessary washing, that he recollected the need that he should punish Eppie, and "make her remember." The idea that she might run away again and come to harm, gave him unusual resolution, and for the first time he determined to try the coal hole—a small closet near the hearth.

"Naughty, naughty Eppie," he suddenly began, holding her on his knee, and pointing to her muddy feet and clothes. "Naughty to cut with the scissors and run away. Eppie must go into the coal hole for being naughty. Daddy must put her in the coal hole."

He half-expected that this would be shock enough, and that Eppie would begin to cry. But instead of that, she began to shake herself on his knee, as if the idea were exciting. Seeing that he must carry out his word, he put her into the coal hole, and held the door closed, with a trembling sense that he was using a strong measure. For a moment there was silence, but then came a little cry, "Opy, opy!" and Silas let her out again, saying, "Now Eppie will never be naughty again, else she must go in the coal hole—a black naughty place."

The weaving must stand still a long while this morning, for now Eppie must be washed, and have clean clothes on. It was to be hoped that this punishment would have a lasting effect, and save time in future—though, perhaps, it would have been better if Eppie had cried more.

In half an hour she was clean again, and Silas, having turned his back to see what he could do with the linen band, threw it down again, with the reflection that Eppie would be good without fastening for the rest of the morning. He turned round again, and was going to place her in her little chair near the loom, when she peeped out at him with black face and hands again, and said, "Eppie in de toal hole!"

This total failure of the coal hole discipline

shook Silas's belief in the effectiveness of punishment. "She'd take it all for fun," he observed to Dolly, "if I didn't hurt her, and that I can't do, Mrs. Winthrop. If she makes me a bit o' trouble, I can bear it. And she's got no tricks that she won't grow out of."

"Well, that's partly true, Master Marner," said Dolly, sympathetically. "And if you can't frighten her off touching things, you must do what you can to keep 'em out of her way. That's what I do wi' the pups as the lads are always rearing. They will worry and gnaw, if it was one's Sunday cap hung anywhere so they could drag it. They know no difference, God help 'em. It's the pushing o' the teeth as sets 'em on, that's what it is."

So Eppie was reared without punishment, the burden of her misdeeds being borne by father Silas. The stone hut was made a soft nest for her, lined with downy patience. And in the world that lay beyond the stone hut she knew nothing of frowns and denials.

Despite the difficulty of carrying her and his yarn or linen at the same time, Silas took her with him in most of his journeys to the farmhouses, unwilling to leave her behind at Dolly Winthrop's, who was always ready to take care of her. Little curly-headed Eppie, the weaver's child, became an object of interest at several outlying homesteads, as well as in the village. Before he had been treated very much as if he had been a useful gnome or brownie—a queer creature with whom one made all greetings and bargains as brief as possible, but who must occasionally have a present of pork or garden stuff to carry home with him, seeing that without him there was no getting the yarn woven. But now Silas met with open smiling faces and cheerful questioning, as a person whose satisfactions and difficulties could be understood. Everywhere he must sit a little and talk about the child, and words of interest were always ready for him.

"Ah, Master Marner, you'll be lucky if she takes the measles soon and easy!"—or, "Why, there isn't many lone men that would want to take up with a little un like that: but I reckon the weaving makes you handier than men that do outdoor work. You're partly as handy as a woman, for weaving comes next to spinning." Elderly masters and mistresses, seated observantly in large kitchen arm chairs, shook their heads over the difficulties of rearing children. They felt Eppie's round arms and legs, pronounced them remarkably firm, and told Silas that, if she turned out well it would be a fine thing for him to have a steady lass when he got helpless. Servant maidens were fond of carrying her out to look at the hens and chickens, or to see if any cherries could be shaken down in the orchard. The small boys and girls approached her slowly, like little dogs face to face with one of their own kind, and eventually gave her kisses. No child was afraid of approaching Silas when Eppie was near him. There was no repulsion around him now, either for young or old, for the little child linked him once more with the whole world. There was love between him and the child that combined them into one, and there was love between the child and the world—from men and women with parental looks and tones, to the red ladybirds and the round pebbles.

Silas began now to think of Raveloe life entirely in relation to Eppie. She must have everything that was good in Raveloe. So he listened, that he might come to understand better what this life was, from which, for fifteen years, he had stood aloof. The inclination to hoard had been utterly crushed at the very first by the loss of his long-stored gold. The coins he earned afterward seemed as irrelevant as stones brought to complete a house suddenly buried by an earthquake. And now something had come to replace his hoard that gave a growing purpose to the earnings, drawing his hope and joy continually onward beyond the money.

In old days there were angels who came and

took men by the hand and led them away from the city of destruction. We see no white-winged angels now. But yet men are led away from threatening destruction: a hand is put into theirs, which leads them forth gently toward a calm and bright land, so that they look backward no more. The hand may be a little child's.

Chapter 15

There was one person, as you will believe, who watched the prosperous growth of Eppie with keener though more hidden interest than any other. He dared not do anything that would imply a stronger interest in a poor man's adopted child than could be expected from the kindliness of the young Squire, when a chance meeting suggested a little present to a simple old fellow whom others noticed with goodwill. But he told himself that the time would come when he might do something toward furthering the welfare of his daughter without incurring suspicion. Was he very uneasy in the meantime at his inability to give his daughter her birthright? It does not appear that he was. The child was being taken care of, and would very likely be happy, as people in humble stations often were—happier, perhaps, than those brought up in luxury.

Godfrey Cass's cheek and eye were brighter than ever now. He was so devoted in his purpose that he seemed like a man of firmness. No Dunsey had come back: people had made up their minds that he was gone for a soldier, or gone "out of the country." Godfrey had ceased to see the shadow of Dunsey across his path, and the path now lay straight. Everybody said Mr. Godfrey had taken the right turn. It was pretty clear what would be the end of things, for there were not many days in the week that he was not seen riding to the Warrens. Godfrey himself, when he was asked if the day had been fixed, smiled with the happiness of a lover who could say "yes," if he liked. He felt a reformed man, delivered from temptation. The vision of his future life seemed to him as a promised land for which he had no cause to fight. He saw himself with all his happiness centered on his own hearth, while Nancy would smile on him as he played with the children.

And that other child—not on the hearth—he would not forget her. He would see that she was well provided for. That was a father's duty.

Chapter 16

It was a bright autumn Sunday, sixteen years after Silas Marner had found his new treasure on the hearth. The bells of the old Raveloe church were ringing the cheerful peal at the end of the morning service. Out of the arched doorway, delayed by friendly greetings and questions, came the richer parishioners who had chosen this bright Sunday morning for churchgoing. It was the rural fashion of that time for the more important members of the congregation to depart first, while their humbler neighbors waited and looked on, stroking their bent heads or dropping their curtsies to any large ratepayer who turned to notice them.

Among these well-clad people, there are some whom we shall recognize, in spite of

Time, who has laid his hand on them all. The tall blond man of forty is not much changed from the Godfrey Cass of twenty-six. He is only fuller in flesh, and has only lost the indefinable look of youth. Perhaps the pretty woman, not much younger than he, who is leaning on his arm, is more changed than her husband. The lovely bloom that used to be always on her cheek now comes occasionally, with the fresh morning air or with some strong surprise.

Yet for all who love human faces best for what they tell of human experience, Nancy's beauty has a heightened interest. Often the soul ripens into fuller goodness while age has spread an ugly film, so that mere glances can never see the preciousness of the fruit. But the years have not been so cruel to Nancy. The firm yet placid mouth, the clear brown eyes, speak now of a nature that has kept its highest qualities. Even the costume, with its dainty neatness and purity, has more significance now that the flirtations of youth have nothing to do with it.

Mr. and Mrs. Godfrey Cass (any higher title has died away since the old Squire died and his inheritance was divided) have turned round to look for the tall aged man and the plainly dressed woman who are a little behind, Nancy wanting to wait for "Father and Priscilla." Now they all turn into a narrower path leading across the churchyard to a small gate opposite the Red House.

It is impossible to mistake Silas Marner. His large brown eyes have a less vague, more responsive gaze. But in everything else one sees signs of aging over the last sixteen years. The weaver has bent shoulders and white hair, though he is not more than fifty-five. But there is the freshest blossom of youth close by his side—a blonde dimpled girl of eighteen, who has vainly tried to tame her curly auburn hair into smoothness under her brown bonnet. The hair ripples as obstinately as a brook under the March breeze, and the little ringlets burst away from the restraining comb behind and show themselves below the bonnet crown. Eppie cannot help being rather vexed about her hair, for there is no other girl in Raveloe who has hair at all like it, and she thinks hair ought to be smooth. She does not like to be blameworthy even in small things.

That good-looking young fellow, in a new suit, who walks behind her, doesn't want Eppie's hair to be different. She surely guesses that there is someone behind her who is thinking about her very particularly, and mustering courage to come to her side as soon as they are out in the lane. Else why should she look rather shy, and take care not to turn away her head from her father Silas, to whom she keeps murmuring little sentences?

"I wish we had a little garden, Father, with double daisies in, like Mrs. Winthrop's," said Eppie, when they were out in the lane. "Only they say it would take a deal of digging and bringing fresh soil—and you couldn't do that, could you, Father? Anyhow, I shouldn't like you to do it, for it 'ud be too hard work for you."

"Yes, I could do it, child, if you want a bit o' garden. These long evenings, I could work at taking in a little bit o' soil, just enough for a root or two o' flowers for you. In the morning, I could have a turn wi' the spade before I sat down to the loom. Why didn't you tell me before that you wanted a bit o' garden?"

"I can dig it for you, Master Marner," said the young man, who was now by Eppie's side, entering into the conversation without the trouble of formalities. "It'll be easy for me after I've done my day's work, or any odd bits o' time when the work's slack. And I'll bring you some soil from Mr. Cass's garden—he'll let me."

"Eh, Aaron, my lad, are you there?" said Silas. "I wasn't aware of you. When Eppie's talking o' things, I see nothing but what she's saying. Well, if you could help me with the digging, we might get her a bit o' garden all the sooner."

"Then, if you think well and good," said

Aaron, "I'll come to the Stone Pits this afternoon, and we'll settle what land's to be taken in, and I'll get up an hour earlier i' the morning, and begin on it."

"But not if you don't promise me not to work at the hard digging, Father," said Eppie. "For I shouldn't ha' said anything about it," she added, half-bashfully, "only Mrs. Winthrop said that Aaron would help, and—"

"And you might ha' known it without Mother telling you," said Aaron. "And Master Marner knows too, I hope, that I'm able and willing to do a turn o' work for him."

"There, now, Father, you won't work in it till it's all easy," said Eppie, "and you and me can mark out the beds, and make holes and plant the roots. It'll be a deal livelier at the Stone Pits when we've got some flowers, for I always think the flowers can see us and know what we're talking about. And I'll have a bit o' rosemary, and bergamot, and thyme, because they're so sweet smelling. But there's lavender only in the gentlefolks' gardens, I think."

"That's no reason that you shouldn't have some," said Aaron, "for I can bring you slips of anything. I'm forced to cut the ends of 'em when I'm gardening, and throw 'em away mostly. There's a big bed o' lavender at the Red House: the missis is very fond of it."

"Well," said Silas, gravely, "as long as you don't ask for anything that is worth much at the Red House. Mr. Cass's been so good to us, and built us the new end o' the cottage, and given us beds and things, as I couldn't abide to be imposing for garden stuff or anything else."

"No, no, there's no imposin'," said Aaron. "There was never a garden in all the parish with such endless waste. It's what I think to myself sometimes, that nobody would run short o' food if the land was made the most of. It sets one thinking o' that—gardening does. But I must go back now, else mother will be upset that I aren't there."

"Bring her with you this afternoon, Aaron," said Eppie. "I don't want to start the garden without her knowing everything from the first—right, Father?"

"Aye, bring her if you can, Aaron," said Silas. "She's sure to have a word to say to help us set things on their right end."

Aaron turned back up to the village, while Silas and Eppie went on down the lonely sheltered lane.

"O Daddy!" she began, when they were in privacy, clasping and squeezing Silas's arm, and skipping round to give him an energetic kiss. "My little old daddy! I'm so glad. I don't think I shall want anything else when we've got a little garden.

I knew Aaron would dig it for us," she went on with roguish triumph. "I knew that very well."

"You're a little devil, you are," said Silas, with mild passive happiness in his face. "But you'll make yourself fine and indebted to Aaron."

"Oh, no, I shan't," said Eppie, laughing and frisking.

"Come, come, let me carry your prayer book, else you'll be dropping it, jumping i' that way."

Eppie was now aware that her behavior was under observation, but it was only the observation of a friendly donkey, browsing with a log fastened to his foot. He was a meek donkey, not scornfully critical of human behavior, but thankful to share in it, if possible, by getting his nose rubbed. Eppie gave him her usual attention, and he followed them, painfully, up to the very door of their home.

But the sound of a sharp bark inside, as Eppie put the key in the door, made him limp away again. The sharp bark was the sign of an excited welcome that was awaiting them from a knowing brown terrier. After dancing at their legs in a hysterical manner, he rushed with a worrying noise at a tortoise-shell kitten under the loom, and then rushed back with a sharp bark again, as if to say, "I have done my duty by this feeble creature, you see." The mother of the kitten sat sunning her white bosom in the window, and looked round with a sleepy air of expecting caresses, though she was not going to take any trouble for them.

This happy animal life was not the only change in the stone cottage. There was no bed now in the living room, and the small space was well filled with decent furniture, all bright and clean enough to satisfy Dolly Winthrop's eye. The oaken table and three-cornered oaken chair were never seen in so poor a cottage. They had come, with the beds and other things, from the Red House. Mr. Godfrey Cass, as everyone said in the village, did very kindly by the weaver. It was only right a man should be helped by those who could afford it, when he had brought up an orphan child, and been father and mother to her—and had lost his money too, so that he had nothing but what he worked for week by week. Nobody was jealous of the weaver, for he was regarded as an exceptional person, whose claims on neighborly help were not to be matched in Raveloe. Any superstition that remained concerning him had taken an entirely new color. Mr. Macey, now a very feeble old man of eighty-six, never seen except in his chimney corner or sitting in the sunshine at his door sill, said that when a man had done what Silas had done for an orphan child, it was a sign that his money would come to light again, or leastwise that the robber would be made to answer for it.

Silas sat down now and watched Eppie with a satisfied gaze as she spread the clean cloth, and set on it the potato pie, warmed up slowly in a safe Sunday fashion, by being put into a dry pot over a slowly dying fire, as the best substitute for an oven. For Silas would not consent to have a grate and oven added to his conveniences. He loved the old brick hearth as he had loved his brown pot—and was it not there when he had found Eppie?

Silas ate his dinner more silently than usual, soon laying down his knife and fork, and watching Eppie play with Snap and the cat. Eppie, with the rippling radiance of her hair and the whiteness of her skin set off by the dark-blue cotton gown, laughed merrily as the kitten held on with her four claws to one shoulder, like a design for a jug handle. Meanwhile, Snap on the right hand and Puss on the other put up their paws toward a morsel that she held out of the reach of both. Finally, Eppie relented, caressed them both, and divided the morsel between them.

But at last, glancing at the clock, she stopped the play, and said, "O Daddy, you're wanting to go into the sunshine to smoke your pipe. But I must clear away first, so as the house may be tidy when Godmother comes. I'll make haste—I won't be long."

Silas had taken to smoking a pipe daily during the last two years, having been strongly urged to it by the sages of Raveloe, as a practice "good for the fits." This advice was sanctioned by Dr. Kimble, on the grounds that it was fine to try what could do no harm. Silas did not highly enjoy smoking, and often wondered how his neighbors could be so fond of it. But accepting what was held to be good had become part of his new self, which had developed in him since he had found Eppie on his hearth. By seeking what Eppie needed, by sharing the effect that everything produced on her, he had himself adopted the customs and beliefs of Raveloe life. He had also begun to ponder the elements of his old faith, and blend them with his new impressions, till he recovered a sense of unity between his past and present.

As it grew easier for him to open his mind to Dolly Winthrop, he gradually communicated to her all he could describe of his early life. The communication was necessarily a slow and difficult process, for Silas's meager power of explanation was not aided by any skill of interpretation in Dolly, whose narrow experience gave her no key to strange customs, and made every novelty a source of wonder, which greatly slowed the story. It was only by fragments, and at intervals which left Dolly time to think about what she had heard, that Silas at last arrived at the climax of the sad story: the drawing of lots, and its false testimony concerning him. This had to be repeated in several interviews, with new questions about this plan for detecting the guilty and clearing the innocent.

"And yours is the same Bible, you're sure o' that, Master Marner—the Bible you brought wi' you from that country—it's the same as what they've got at church, and what Eppie's learning to read in?"

"Yes," said Silas, "every bit the same. There's drawing o' lots in the Bible, mind you," he added in a lower tone.

"Oh, dear, dear," said Dolly in a grieved voice, as if she were hearing an unfavorable report of a sick man's case. She was silent for some minutes; at last she said, "I can never rightly know the meaning o' what I hear at church, only a bit here and there, but I know it's good words—I do. But what lies upo' your mind—it's this, Master Marner: if Them above had done the right thing by you, They'd never ha' let you be turned out for a wicked thief when you was innocent."

"Ah!" said Silas, who had now come to understand Dolly's way of speaking, "that was what fell on me like a red-hot iron; because, you see, there was nobody who cared for me above or below. And him I'd been friends with for ten year and more, since when we was lads—mine own familiar friend in whom I trusted, had lifted up his heel against me, and worked to ruin me."

"Eh, but he was a bad one—I can't think as there's another such," said Dolly. "But I'm o'ercome, Master Marner, as if I'd waked and didn't know whether it was night or morning. I feel somehow sure that there was a rights in what happened to you, if one could but make it out. You'd no call to lose heart as you did. But we'll talk on it again. Sometimes things come into my head when I'm leeching or poulticing, as I could never think on when I was sitting still."

Dolly was too useful a woman not to have many opportunities of illumination of the kind she referred to, and it was not long before she returned to the subject.

"Master Marner," she said, one day that she came to bring home Eppie's washing, "I've been sore puzzled for a good bit wi' that trouble o' yours and the drawing o' lots. But it come to me all clear like, that night when I was sitting up wi' poor Bessy Fawkes, who is dead and left her children behind, God help 'em. It come to me as clear as daylight. But whether I've got hold on it now, or can anyways bring it to my tongue's end, that I don't know. For I've often a deal inside me that will never come out. Your folks in your old country never saying prayers by heart nor saying 'em out of a book, they must be wonderful clever. If I didn't know "Our Father," and little bits o' good words as I can carry out o' church wi' me, I might go down o' my knees every night, but nothing could I say."

"But you can usually say something that I can make sense of, Mrs. Winthrop," said Silas.

"Well, then, Master Marner, it come to me like this: I can make nothing o' the drawing o' lots and the answer coming wrong. But what come to me as clear as the daylight, that Them above has got a deal tenderer heart than what I've got—for I can't be anyways better than Them that made me. If anything looks hard to me, it's because there's things I don't know of. And so, while I was thinking o' that, you come into my mind, Master Marner, and it all come pouring in. If I felt i' my inside what was the right and just thing by you, and them as prayed and drawed the lots, if they'd ha' done the right thing by you if they could, isn't there Them that made us, and knows better and has a better will? And that's all I can be sure of, and everything else is a big puzzle to me when I think on it. For there was the fever come and took off them who were full-grown, and left the helpless children; and there's the breaking o' limbs. Eh, there's trouble i' this world, and there's things that we can never understand. And all we've got to do is to trust, Master Marner—to do the right thing as far as we know, and to trust. For if us that knows so little can see a bit o' good, we may be sure that there's a good bigger than what we can know. I feel it inside that it must be so. And if you could ha' gone on trusting, Master Marner, you wouldn't ha' run away from your fellow creatures and been so alone."

"Ah, but that would ha' been hard," said Silas, in an undertone. "It would ha' been hard to trust then."

"And so it would," said Dolly, almost with regret. "Them things are easier said than done. I'm partly ashamed o' talking."

"Nay, nay," said Silas, "you're i' the right, Mrs. Winthrop—you're i' the right. There's good i' this world—I've a feeling o' that now. It makes a man feel as there's a good more than he can see, i' spite o' the trouble and the wickedness. That drawing o' the lots is dark, but the child was sent to me: there's dealings with us—there's dealings."

This dialogue took place in Eppie's earlier years, when Silas had to part with her for two hours every day, that she might learn to read at the dame school. Now that she was grown up, Silas had often been led, in those moments of quiet outpouring that come to people who live together in perfect love, to talk with her too of the past, and how and why he had been a lonely man until she had been sent to him. For it would have been impossible for him to hide from Eppie that she was not his own child. Even if people did not gossip in Raveloe, her own questions about her mother could not have been avoided. So Eppie had long known how her mother had died on the snowy ground, and how she herself had been found on the hearth by father Silas, who had taken her golden curls for his lost guineas brought back to him. The tender and peculiar love with which Silas had reared her in almost inseparable companionship with himself, aided by the seclusion of their dwelling, had preserved her from the lowering influences of the village talk and habits, and had kept her mind fresh. So it is not surprising if, in other things besides her delicate prettiness, she was not quite a common village maiden, but had a touch of refinement.

She was too childish and simple to ask questions about her unknown father. For a long while it did not even occur to her that she must have had a father. The first time that the idea of her mother having had a husband presented itself to her, was when Silas showed her the wedding ring which had been taken from the wasted finger, and had been carefully preserved by him in a little lacquered box shaped like a shoe. He gave it to Eppie when she had grown up, and she often opened it to look at the ring. But still she thought hardly at all about the father of whom it was the symbol. Had she not a father very close to her, who loved her better than any real fathers in the village seemed to love their daughters?

However, who her mother was, and how she came to die, were questions that often pressed on Eppie's mind. Her knowledge of Mrs. Winthrop, who was her nearest friend next to Silas, made her feel that a mother must be very precious. She had again and again asked Silas to tell her how her mother looked, and how he had found her against the furze bush, led toward it by the little footsteps and the outstretched arms. The furze bush was there still. This afternoon, when Eppie came out with Silas into the sunshine, it was the first object that caught her eye.

"Father," she said, in a serious tone, "we shall take the furze bush into the garden. It'll go into the corner, and just against it I'll put snowdrops and crocuses, 'cause Aaron says they won't die out, but will always grow more and more."

"Ah, child," said Silas, always ready to talk when he had his pipe in his hand, apparently enjoying the pauses more than the puffs. "It wouldn't do to ignore the furze bush. There's nothing prettier, to my thinking, when it's yellow with flowers. But it's just come into my head that we need a fence—maybe Aaron can help us. A fence we must have, else the donkeys and things will come and trample everything down. And fencing's hard, by what I can make out."

"Oh, I'll tell you, Daddy," said Eppie, clasping her hands suddenly, after a minute's thought. "There's lots o' loose stones about, some of 'em not big, and we might lay 'em atop of one another, and make a wall. You and me could carry the smallest, and Aaron 'ud carry the rest—I know he would."

"Eh, my precious un," said Silas, "there isn't enough stones to go all round. As for you carrying, why, wi' your little arms you couldn't carry a stone bigger than a turnip. You're delicate made, my dear," he added, with a tender intonation. "That's what Mrs. Winthrop says."

"Oh, I'm stronger than you think, Daddy," said Eppie. "If there wasn't stones enough to go all round, why they'll go part o' the way, and then it'll be easier to get sticks and things for the rest. See here, round the big pit, how many stones!"

She skipped forward to the pit, meaning to lift one of the stones and exhibit her strength, but she started back in surprise.

"Oh, Father, just come and look here," she exclaimed. "Come and see how the water's gone down since yesterday. Why, yesterday the pit was ever so full!"

"Well, to be sure," said Silas, coming to her side. "Why, that's the draining they've begun, since harvest, i' Mr. Osgood's fields, I reckon. The foreman said to me the other day, when I passed by 'em, 'Master Marner,' he said, 'I shouldn't wonder if we lay your bit o' waste as dry as a bone.' It was Mr. Godfrey Cass, he said, was behind the draining: he's bought these fields o' Mr. Osgood."

"How odd it'll seem to have the old pit dried up!" said Eppie, turning away, and stooping to lift rather a large stone. "See, Daddy, I can carry this quite well," she said, going along with much energy for a few steps, but soon letting it fall.

"Ah, you're fine and strong, aren't you?" said Silas, while Eppie shook her aching arms and laughed. "Come, come, let us go and sit down on the bank against the stile there, and have no more lifting. You might hurt yourself, child. You need somebody to work for you— and my arm isn't over strong."

Silas uttered the last sentence slowly, as if it implied more than met the ear. Eppie, when they sat down on the bank, nestled close to his side, and, taking hold caressingly of the arm that was not over strong, held it on her lap, while

Silas puffed again dutifully at the pipe, which occupied his other arm. An ash in the hedgerow behind made a screen from the sun, and threw happy playful shadows all about them.

"Father," said Eppie, very gently, after they had been sitting in silence a little while, "if I was to be married, ought I to be married with my mother's ring?"

Silas gave an almost imperceptible start, and then said, in a subdued tone, "Why, Eppie, have you been thinking on it?"

"Only this last week, Father," said Eppie, "since Aaron talked to me about it."

"And what did he say?" said Silas, still in the same subdued way.

"He said he should like to be married, because he was going on twenty-four, and had got a deal of gardening work, now that Mr. Mott's given up. He goes twice a week regular to Mr. Cass's, and once to Mr. Osgood's, and they're going to take him on at the Rectory."

"And who is it he's wanting to marry?" said Silas, with rather a sad smile.

"Why, me, to be sure, Daddy," said Eppie, with dimpling laughter, kissing her father's cheek. "As if he'd want to marry anybody else!"

"And you mean to have him, do you?" said Silas.

"Yes, sometime," said Eppie. "I don't know

when. Everybody's married sometime, Aaron says. But I told him that wasn't true. I said, look at Father—he's never been married."

"No, child," said Silas, "your father was a lone man till you was sent to him."

"But you'll never be lone again, Father," said Eppie, tenderly. "That was what Aaron said—'I could never think o' taking you away from Master Marner, Eppie.' And I said, 'It 'ud be no use if you did, Aaron.' And he wants us all to live together, so you needn't work a bit, Father, only what's for your own pleasure. He'd be as good as a son to you—that was what he said."

"And should you like that, Eppie?" said Silas, looking at her.

"I shouldn't mind it, Father," said Eppie, quite simply. "And I should like things to be so that you needn't work much. But if it wasn't for that, I'd sooner things didn't change. I'm very happy. I like Aaron to be fond of me, and come and see us often, and behave pretty to you—he always does behave pretty to you, doesn't he, Father?"

"Yes, child, nobody could behave better," said Silas, emphatically. "He's his mother's lad."

"But I don't want any change," said Eppie. "I should like to go on a long, long while, just as we are. Only Aaron does want a change. He

made me cry a bit—only a bit—because he said
I didn't care for him, for if I cared for him I
should want us to be married, as he did."

"Eh, my blessed child," said Silas, laying
down his pipe as if it were useless to pretend to
smoke any longer. "We'll ask Aaron's mother
what she thinks: if there's a right thing to do,
she'll come at it. But there's this to be thought
on, Eppie: things will change, whether we like it
or no. Things won't go on for a long while just
as they are and no difference. I shall get older
and more helpless, and be a burden on you, if I
don't go away from you altogether. Not that I
mean you'd think me a burden—I know you
wouldn't—but it 'ud be hard upon you. When I
think about that, I like to think you'd have
somebody else besides me—somebody young
and strong, that will outlast your own life, and
take care of you to the end." Silas paused, and,
resting his wrists on his knees, lifted his hands
up and down meditatively as he looked on the
ground.

"Then, would you like me to be married,
Father?" said Eppie, with a little trembling in
her voice.

"I'll not be the man to say no, Eppie," said
Silas, emphatically. "But we'll ask your godmother. She'll wish the right thing by you and
her son too."

"There they come, then," said Eppie. "Let us go and meet 'em. Oh, the pipe! Won't you have it lit again, Father?" said Eppie, lifting that medicinal appliance from the ground.

"Nay, child," said Silas, "I've done enough for today. I think, maybe, a little of it does me more good than so much at once."

Chapter 17

While Silas and Eppie sat on the bank discoursing in the shade of the ash tree, Miss Priscilla Lammeter was resisting her sister's arguments that it would be better to take tea at the Red House and let her father have a long nap, than drive home to the Warrens so soon after dinner. The family party of four was seated round the table in the dark parlor, with the Sunday dessert before them, of fresh hazelnuts, apples, and pears.

A great change had come over the parlor since we saw it in Godfrey's bachelor days, and under the wifeless reign of the old Squire. Now all is polished, and yesterday's dust is never allowed to rest, from the oaken boards round the carpet, to the old Squire's gun and whips and walking sticks, resting on the stag's antlers above the mantelpiece. All other signs of sporting and outdoor occupation Nancy has removed to another room. But she preserves sacredly in a place of honor these relics of her husband's departed father. The tankards are on the side table still, but the silver is undimmed by handling, and there are no dregs to send forth unpleasant smells. The only prevailing scent is of the lavender and rose leaves that fill the vases. All is purity and order in this once dreary room, for, fifteen years ago, a new authority entered.

"Now, father," said Nancy, "is there any call for you to go home to tea? May you just as well stay with us? Such a beautiful evening it's likely to be."

The old gentleman had been talking with Godfrey about the increasing number of poor and the ruinous times, and had not heard his daughters' conversation.

"My dear, you must ask Priscilla," he said, in the once firm voice, now rather broken. "She manages me and the farm too."

"And good reason I should manage you, father," said Priscilla, "else you'd be giving yourself your death with rheumatism. And as for the farm, if anything turns out wrong, as it can't help do in these times, there's nothing kills a man so soon as having nobody to blame but himself. It's the best way o' being master, to let somebody else do the ordering, and keep the blaming in your own hands. It 'ud save many a man a stroke, I believe."

"Well, well, my dear," said her father, with a quiet laugh, "I didn't say you don't manage for everybody's good."

"Then manage to stay for tea, Priscilla," said Nancy, putting her hand on her sister's arm affectionately. "Come now. We'll go round the garden while Father has his nap."

"My dear child, he'll have a beautiful nap in the gig, for I shall drive. And as for staying for tea, I can't hear of it. The dairymaid, now she knows she's to be married, would as soon pour the new milk into the pig trough as into the pans. That's the way with 'em all. It's as if they thought the world 'ud be new-made because they're to be married. So come and let me put my bonnet on, and there'll be time for us to walk round the garden while the horse is being put in."

When the sisters were treading the neatly swept garden walks, between the bright turf that contrasted pleasantly with the dark hedges, Priscilla said, "I'm as glad as anything at your husband's making that exchange o' land with cousin Osgood, and beginning the dairying. It's a thousand pities you didn't do it before, for it'll give you something to fill your mind. There's nothing like a dairy if folks want a bit o' worry to make the days pass. As for rubbing furniture, when you can see your face in a table there's nothing else to look for. But there's always something fresh with the dairy. Even in the depths o' winter there's some pleasure in conquering the butter. My dear," added Priscilla, pressing her sister's hand affectionately as they walked side by side, "you'll never be low when you've got a dairy."

"Ah, Priscilla," said Nancy, returning the pressure with a grateful glance of her clear eyes, "but it won't make it up to Godfrey: a dairy's not so much to a man. And it's only what he cares for that ever makes me low. I'm contented with the blessings we have, if he could be contented."

"It drives me past patience," said Priscilla, impetuously, "that way o' the men. Always wanting and wanting, and never easy with what they've got. They can't sit comfortable in their chairs when they've neither ache nor pain, but either they must stick a pipe in their mouths, to make 'em better than well, or else they must be swallowing something strong before the next meal comes in. But our father was never that sort o' man. And if it had pleased God to make you ugly, like me, so as the men wouldn't ha' run after you, we might have kept to our own family, and had nothing to do with folks that have got uneasy blood in their veins."

"Oh, don't say so, Priscilla," said Nancy, regretting that she had called forth this outburst. "Nobody has any occasion to find fault with Godfrey. It's natural he should be disappointed at not having any children. Every man likes to have somebody to work for and lay by for, and he always counted on making a fuss with 'em when they were little. There's many another man that would hanker more than he does. He's the best of husbands."

"Oh, I know," said Priscilla, smiling sarcastically. "I know the way o' wives. They set one on to abuse their husbands, and then they turn round on one and praise 'em as if they wanted to sell 'em. But Father'll be waiting for me. We must turn now."

The large carriage with the steady old gray was at the front door, and Mr. Lammeter was already on the stone steps, passing the time in recalling to Godfrey how very fine Speckle looked when his master used to ride him.

"I always would have a good horse, you know," said the old gentleman, liking to remind his juniors of that spirited time.

"Mind you bring Nancy to the Warrens before the week's out, Mr. Cass," was Priscilla's parting injunction, as she took the reins, and shook them gently, by way of friendly incitement to Speckle.

"I shall just take a turn to the fields against the Stone Pits, Nancy, and look at the draining," said Godfrey.

"You'll be in again by tea time, dear?"

"Oh, yes, I shall be back in an hour."

It was Godfrey's custom on a Sunday afternoon to do a little contemplative farming in a leisurely walk. Nancy seldom accompanied him. The women of her generation—unless, like Priscilla, they took to outdoor management—were not given to much walking beyond their own house and garden, finding sufficient exercise in domestic duties. So, when Priscilla was not with her, she usually sat with the Bible before her, and after following the text with her eyes for a little while, she would gradually permit them to wander as her thoughts had already insisted on wandering.

But Nancy's Sunday thoughts were rarely less than devout. She was not educated enough to relate the sacred documents of the past with her own obscure, simple life. But the spirit of integrity, and the sense of responsibility for the effect of her conduct on others, which were strong elements in Nancy's character, had made it a habit with her to scrutinize her past feelings and actions.

She filled the vacant moments by living inwardly, again and again, through all her remembered experience, especially through the fifteen years of her married time. She recalled the times that had given her a deeper insight into the relations and trials of life, or that had tried her patience, or tested her sense of duty. All the while she asked herself whether she had been to blame in any respect. This excessive self-questioning may have resulted from a lack of outward activity, particularly that of mother-hood. "I can do so little—have I done it all well?" was her recurring thought.

There was one main thread of painful experience in Nancy's married life, revisited often. The first wandering of her thought from the text, which she still attempted dutifully to follow with her eyes and silent lips, was about her deepest wounds. She believed that the absence of children from their hearth was unbearable to her husband.

Yet sweet Nancy might have been expected to feel worse at the denial of this blessing. Was there not a drawer filled with the neat work of her hands, all unworn and untouched, just as she had arranged it there fourteen years ago—but for one little dress, which had been made the burial dress? But under this trial Nancy was so firmly stalwart, that years ago she had suddenly renounced the habit of visiting this drawer.

Perhaps it was this very severity toward her

own indulgence that made her so lenient with her husband. "It is very different—it is much worse for a man to be disappointed in that way: a woman can always be satisfied with devoting herself to her husband, but a man wants something that will make him look forward more— and sitting by the fire is so much duller to him than to a woman." Always, when Nancy reached this point—trying, with sympathy, to see everything as Godfrey saw it—she questioned herself yet again. Had she done everything in her power to make Godfrey feel better? Had she really been right to deny her husband's wish that they should adopt a child?

To adopt a child, because children of your own had been denied you, was to try to change your fate. The adopted child, she was convinced, would never turn out well, and would be a curse to those who had rebelliously sought what it was clear that, for some high reason, they were better without. When you saw a thing was not meant to be, said Nancy, it was your duty not to even wish for it. For example, she would have given up shopping at a particular place if, on three successive times, rain, or some other cause of Heaven, had formed an obstacle. She would have expected a broken limb or other heavy misfortune to anyone who persisted in spite of such signs.

"But why should you think the child would turn out ill?" said Godfrey. "She has thrived as well as a child can do with the weaver, and he adopted her. There isn't such a pretty little girl anywhere else in the parish, or one fitter for the life we could give her. How could she be a curse to anybody?"

"Yes, my dear Godfrey," said Nancy, who was sitting with her hands tightly clasped together, and with yearning, regretful affection in her eyes. "The child may not turn out ill with the weaver. But, then, he didn't go to seek her, as we should be doing. It will be wrong. I feel sure it will. Don't you remember what that lady we met at the Royston Baths told us about the child her sister adopted? That was the only adopting I ever heard of, and the child died when it was twenty-three. Dear Godfrey, don't ask me to do what I know is wrong, for I should never be happy again. I know it's very hard for you—it's easier for me—but it's the will of Providence."

Godfrey had from the first picked Eppie, then about twelve years old, as a child suitable for them to adopt. It had never occurred to him that Silas would rather part with his life than with Eppie. Surely the weaver would wish the best to the child he had taken so much trouble with, and would be glad that such good fortune should happen to her. She would always be very grateful to him, and he would be well provided for to the end of his life. Was it not an appropriate thing for people in a higher station to take a burden off the hands of a man in a lower? This was rather a coarse way of understanding Silas's relation to Eppie. But Godfrey thought that deep affections could hardly go along with callous palms and poverty, and he did not know very much about the weaver. It was only this lack of knowledge that could have made it possible for Godfrey deliberately to plan an unfeeling project. His natural kindness had outlived his cruelty, and Nancy's praise of him as a husband was not founded entirely on illusion.

"I was right," she said to herself, when she had recalled all their discussion. "I feel I was right to say no to him, though it hurt me more than anything. But how good Godfrey has been about it! Many men would have been very angry with me for denying their wishes. They might have said it was bad luck to marry me. But Godfrey has never been the man to say me an unkind word. He can't hide that everything seems so empty to him, I know. And the land— what a difference it would make to him, when he goes to see after things, if he'd children growing up that he was doing it all for! But perhaps if he'd married a woman who'd have had children, she'd have pained him in other ways."

This possibility was Nancy's chief comfort, and she worked to make it impossible that any other wife should have had more perfect tenderness. Godfrey appreciated her loving effort, and did not made her feel badly about her decision. Indeed, he was in awe of her strong morality and integrity. It seemed to him impossible that he should ever confess to her the truth about Eppie. She would never recover from the repulsion of his earlier marriage, after that long concealment. And the child, too, he thought, must repel her. The shock to Nancy's mingled pride and ignorance of the world's evil might even be too much for her delicate frame. Since he had married her with that secret in his heart, he must keep it there to the last. Whatever else he did, he could not hurt his marriage.

Meanwhile, why could he not accept the absence of children from a hearth brightened by such a wife? Why did his mind fly uneasily to that void, as if it were the sole reason that life was not thoroughly joyous to him? Perhaps it is the way with all men and women who reach middle age not knowing that life can never be thoroughly joyous. In the dull hours, they seek something that they haven't got. In Godfrey's case there were further reasons: his conscience, never easy about Eppie, now saw his childless home as a punishment. As the time passed on, under Nancy's refusal to adopt her, any correction of his error became more and more difficult.

On this Sunday afternoon it was already four years since there had been any reference to the subject between them, and Nancy supposed that it was forever buried.

"I wonder if he'll mind it less or more as he gets older," she thought. "I'm afraid more. Aged people feel the lack of children. What would Father do without Priscilla? And if I die, Godfrey will be very lonely. But I won't be over-anxious. I must do my best for the present."

With that last thought Nancy roused herself from her reverie, and turned her eyes again toward the forgotten page. It had been forgotten longer than she imagined, for she was soon surprised by the appearance of the servant with the tea things. It was, in fact, a little before the usual time for tea, but Jane had her reasons.

"Has your master come into the yard, Jane?"

"No ma'm, he hasn't," said Jane, with a slight emphasis, of which her mistress took no notice.

"I don't know whether you've seen 'em, ma'm," continued Jane, after a pause, "but there's folks making haste all one way, afore the front window. I think something's happened. There's never a man to be seen i' the yard, else I'd send and see. I've been up into the top attic, but there's no seeing anything for trees. I hope nobody's hurt, that's all."

"Oh, no, I daresay there's nothing much the matter," said Nancy. "It's perhaps Mr. Snell's bull got out again, as he did before."

"I hope he didn't gore anybody, that's all," said Jane.

"That girl is always terrifying me," thought Nancy. "I wish Godfrey would come in."

She went to the front window and looked as far as she could see along the road, with an uneasiness that she felt to be childish, for there were now no such signs of excitement as Jane had spoken of. Godfrey would not be likely to return by the village road, but by the fields. She continued to stand, however, looking at the placid churchyard with the long shadows of the gravestones across the bright green hillocks, and at the glowing autumn colors of the Rectory trees beyond. Before such calm external beauty the presence of a vague fear is more distinctly felt—like a raven flapping its slow wings across the sunny air. Nancy wished more and more that Godfrey would come in.

Chapter 18

Someone opened the door at the other end of the room, and Nancy felt that it was her husband. She turned from the window with gladness in her eyes, for the wife's chief dread was stilled.

"Dear, I'm so thankful you're come," she said, going toward him. "I began to get—"

She paused abruptly, for Godfrey was laying down his hat with trembling hands, and turned toward her with a pale face and a strange glance, as if he saw her indeed, but saw her as part of a scene invisible to herself. She laid her hand on his arm, not daring to speak again, but he left the touch unnoticed, and threw himself into his chair.

Jane was already at the door with the hissing urn. "Tell her to keep away, will you?" said

Godfrey. When the door was closed again he exerted himself to speak.

"Sit down, Nancy—there," he said, pointing to a chair opposite him. "I came back as soon as I could, to hinder anybody's telling you but me. I've had a great shock—but I care most about the shock it'll be to you."

"It isn't Father and Priscilla?" said Nancy, with quivering lips, clasping her hands together tightly on her lap.

"No, it's nobody living," said Godfrey. "It's Dunstan—my brother Dunstan, that we lost sight of sixteen years ago. We've found him—found his body—his skeleton."

The deep dread Godfrey's look had created in Nancy made her feel these words a relief. She sat in comparative calmness to hear what else he had to tell. He went on. "The Stone Pit has gone dry suddenly—from the draining, I suppose. There he lies—has lain for sixteen years, wedged between two great stones. There's his watch and seals, and there's my gold-handled hunting whip, with my name on. He took it away, without my knowing, the day he went hunting on Wildfire, the last time he was seen."

Godfrey paused: it was not so easy to say what came next.

"Do you think he drowned himself?" said Nancy, almost wondering that her husband should be so deeply shaken by what had happened all those years ago to an unloved brother, of whom worse things had been imagined.

"No, he fell in," said Godfrey, in a low but distinct voice, as if he felt some deep meaning in the fact. Presently he added, "Dunstan was the man that robbed Silas Marner."

The blood rushed to Nancy's face and neck at this surprise and shame, for she had been brought up to regard even a distant kinship with crime as a dishonor.

"O Godfrey!" she said, with compassion in her tone, for she had immediately realized that the dishonor must be felt still more keenly by her husband.

"There was the money in the pit," he continued—"all the weaver's money. Everything's been gathered up, and they're taking the skeleton to the Rainbow. But I came back to tell you."

He was silent, looking at the floor for two long minutes. Nancy would have said some words of comfort under this disgrace, but she refrained, from an instinctive sense that Godfrey had something else to tell her. Presently he lifted his eyes to her face, and kept them fixed on her, as he said, "Everything comes to light, Nancy, sooner or later. When God Almighty wills it, our secrets are found out. I've lived with a secret on my mind, but I'll keep it from you no longer. I wouldn't have you know it by somebody else, and I wouldn't have you find it out after I'm dead. I'll tell you now. It's been 'I will' and 'I won't' with me all my life—I'll make sure of myself now."

Nancy's utmost dread had returned. The eyes of the husband and wife met with awe in them, as at a crisis that suspended affection.

"Nancy," said Godfrey, slowly, "when I married you, I hid something from you—something I ought to have told you. That woman Marner found dead in the snow—Eppie's mother—that wretched woman—was my wife. Eppie is my child."

He paused, dreading the effect of his confession. But Nancy sat quite still, only that her eyes dropped and ceased to meet his. She was pale and quiet as a meditative statue, clasping her hands on her lap.

"You'll never think the same of me again," said Godfrey, after a little while, with some tremor in his voice.

She was silent.

"I oughtn't to have left the child unclaimed. I oughtn't to have kept it from you. But I couldn't bear to give you up, Nancy. I was led away into marrying her—I suffered for it."

Still Nancy was silent, looking down, and he

almost expected that she would get up and say she would go to her father's. How could she have any mercy for faults that must seem so black to her, with her simple, severe notions?

But at last she lifted up her eyes to his again and spoke. There was no indignation in her voice—only deep regret.

"Godfrey, if you had told me this six years ago, we could have done some of our duty by the child. Do you think I'd have refused to take her in, if I'd known she was yours?"

At that moment Godfrey felt all the bitterness of an error that was not simply futile, but had defeated its own end. He had underestimated this wife with whom he had lived so long. But she spoke again, with more agitation.

"And—Oh, Godfrey—if we'd had her from the first, if you'd taken to her as you ought, she'd have loved me for her mother—and you'd have been happier with me. I could better have borne my little baby dying, and our life might have been more like what we used to think it 'ud be."

The tears fell, and Nancy ceased to speak.

"But you wouldn't have married me then, Nancy, if I'd told you," said Godfrey, urged, in the bitterness of his self-reproach, to prove to himself that his conduct had not been utter folly. "You may think you would now, but you wouldn't then. With your pride and your father's, you'd have hated having anything to do with me after the talk there'd have been."

"I can't say what I should have done about that, Godfrey. I should never have married anybody else. But I wasn't worth doing wrong for—nothing is in this world. Nothing is so good as it seems beforehand—not even our marrying wasn't, you see."

There was a faint sad smile on Nancy's face as she said the last words.

"I'm a worse man than you thought I was, Nancy," said Godfrey, rather tremulously. "Can you forgive me ever?"

"The wrong to me is but little, Godfrey. You've made it up to me—you've been good to me for fifteen years. It's another you did the wrong to, and I doubt it can ever be all made up for."

"But we can take Eppie now," said Godfrey. "I won't mind the world knowing at last. I'll be plain and open for the rest o' my life."

"It'll be different coming to us, now she's grown up," said Nancy, shaking her head sadly. "But it's your duty to acknowledge her and provide for her. And I'll do my part by her, and pray to God Almighty to make her love me."

"Then we'll go together to Silas Marner's this very night, as soon as everything's quiet at the Stone Pits."

Chapter 19

Between eight and nine o'clock that evening, Eppie and Silas sat alone in the cottage. After the great excitement of the events of the afternoon, Silas had felt a longing for this quiet, and had even begged Mrs. Winthrop and Aaron, who had naturally lingered behind everyone else, to leave him alone with his child.

Silas sat in his armchair and looked at Eppie. She had drawn her own chair toward his knees, and leaned forward, holding both his hands, while she looked up at him. On the table near them, lit by a candle, lay the recovered gold—the old long-loved gold, ranged in orderly heaps, as Silas used to range it in the days when it was his only joy. He had been telling her how he used to count it every night, and how his soul was utterly desolate till she was sent to him.

"At first, I'd a sort o' feeling come across me now and then," he was saying in a subdued tone, "as if you might be changed into the gold again. Sometimes, turn my head which way I would, I seemed to see the gold. I thought I should be glad if I could feel it, and find it was come back. But that didn't last long. After a bit, I should have thought it was a curse come again, if it had drove you from me, for I'd got to feel the need o' your looks and your voice and the touch o' your little fingers. You didn't know then, Eppie, when you were such a little un—you didn't know what your old father Silas felt for you."

"But I know now, father," said Eppie. "If it hadn't been for you, they'd have taken me to the workhouse, and there'd have been nobody to love me."

"Eh, my precious child, the blessing was mine. If you hadn't been sent to save me, I should ha' gone to the grave in my misery. The money was taken away from me in time. You see it's been kept—kept till it was wanted for you. It's wonderful—our life is wonderful."

Silas sat in silence a few minutes, looking at the money. "It takes no hold of me now," he said, ponderingly. "The money doesn't. I wonder if it ever could again. It might, if I lost you, Eppie. I might come to think I was forsaken again, and lose the feeling that God was good to me."

At that moment there was a knocking at the door, and Eppie was obliged to rise without answering Silas. Beautiful she looked, with the tenderness of gathering tears in her eyes and a slight flush on her cheeks, as she stepped to open the door. The flush deepened when she saw Mr. and Mrs. Godfrey Cass. She made her little rustic curtsy, and held the door wide for them to enter.

"We're disturbing you very late, my dear," said Mrs. Cass, taking Eppie's hand, and looking in her face with an expression of anxious interest and admiration. Nancy herself was pale and tremulous.

Eppie, after placing chairs for Mr. and Mrs. Cass, went to stand against Silas, opposite to them.

"Well, Marner," said Godfrey, trying to speak with perfect firmness, "it's a great comfort to me to see you with your money again, that you've been deprived of so many years. It was one of my family did you the wrong—the more grief to me—and I feel bound to make up to you for it in every way. Whatever I can do for you will be nothing but paying a debt, even if I looked no further than the robbery. But there are other things I'm beholden—shall be beholden to you for, Marner."

Godfrey checked himself. It had been agreed between him and his wife that the subject of his fatherhood should be approached very carefully, and that, if possible, the disclosure should be reserved for the future, so that it might be made to Eppie gradually. Nancy had urged this, because she felt strongly the painful light in which Eppie must inevitably see the relation between her father and mother.

Silas, always ill at ease when he was being spoken to by "betters," such as Mr. Cass—tall, powerful, florid men, seen chiefly on horseback—answered with some constraint, "Sir, I've a deal to thank you for a'ready. As for the robbery, I count it no loss to me. And if I did, you couldn't help it. You aren't answerable for it."

"You may look at it in that way, Marner, but I never can. I hope you'll let me act according to my own feeling of what's just. I know you're easily contented: you've been a hardworking man all your life."

"Yes, sir, yes," said Marner, meditatively. "I should ha' been bad off without my work. It was what I held by when everything else was gone from me."

"Ah," said Godfrey, applying Marner's words simply to his bodily wants, "it was a good trade for you in this country, because there's been a great deal of linen weaving to be done.

But you're getting rather past such close work, Marner. It's time you laid by and had some rest. You look a good deal pulled down, though you're not an old man, are you?"

"Fifty-five, as near as I can say, sir," said Silas.

"Oh, why, you may live thirty years longer—look at old Macey! And that money on the table, after all, is little. It won't go far either way—whether it's put out to interest, or you were to live on it as long as it would last. It wouldn't go far if you'd nobody to keep but yourself, and you've had two to keep for a good many years now."

"Eh, sir," said Silas, unaffected by anything Godfrey was saying. "I'm in no fear o' want. We shall do very well—Eppie and me 'ull do well enough. There's few working folks have got so much laid by as that. I don't know what it is to gentlefolks, but I look upon it as a deal—almost too much. And as for us, it's little we want."

"Only the garden, Father," said Eppie, blushing up to the ears the moment after.

"You love a garden, do you, my dear?" said Nancy, thinking that this turn in the point of view might help her husband. "We should agree in that. I give a deal of time to the garden."

"Ah, there's plenty of gardening at the Red House," said Godfrey. "You've done a good

part by Eppie, Marner, for sixteen years. It 'ud
be a great comfort to you to see her well provided for, wouldn't it? She looks blooming and
healthy, but not fit for any hardships. She does-
n't look like a strapping girl come of working
parents. You'd like to see her taken care of by
those who can leave her well-off, and make a
lady of her. She's more fit for it than for a rough
life, such as she might come to have in a few
years' time."

A slight flush came over Marner's face, and
disappeared, like a passing gleam. Eppie was
simply wondering that Mr. Cass should talk so
about things that seemed to have nothing to do
with reality. But Silas was hurt and uneasy.

"I don't take your meaning, sir," he
answered.

"Well, my meaning is this, Marner," said
Godfrey, determined to come to the point.
"Mrs. Cass and I, you know, have no children—
nobody to benefit by our good home and everything else we have—more than enough for ourselves. And we should like to have somebody in
the place of a daughter to us—we should like to
have Eppie, and treat her in every way as our
own child. It 'ud be a great comfort to you in
your old age, I hope, to see her fortune made in
that way, after you've taken the trouble of bringing her up so well. And it's right you should

have every reward for that. And Eppie, I'm sure, will always love you and be grateful to you. She'd come and see you very often, and we should all be on the lookout to do everything we could toward making you comfortable."

A plain man like Godfrey Cass, speaking under some embarrassment, necessarily blunders on words that are coarser than his intentions, and that are likely to fall gratingly on susceptible feelings. While he had been speaking, Eppie had quietly passed her arm behind Silas's head, and let her hand rest against it caressingly. She felt him trembling violently. He was silent for some moments when Mr. Cass had ended—powerless under the conflict of emotions, all painful. Eppie's heart was swelling at the sense that her father was in distress. She was just going to lean down and speak to him, when he said, faintly, "Eppie, my child, speak. I won't stand in your way. Thank Mr. and Mrs. Cass."

Eppie took her hand from her father's head, and came forward a step. Her cheeks were flushed, but not with shyness this time. The sense that her father was in doubt and suffering banished that sort of self-consciousness. She dropped a low curtsy, first to Mrs. Cass and then to Mr. Cass, and said, "Thank you, ma'am— thank you, sir. But I can't leave my father. And I don't want to be a lady—thank you all the same. I couldn't give up the folks I've been used to."

Eppie's lips began to tremble a little at the last words. She retreated to her father's chair again, and held him round the neck, while Silas, with a subdued sob, put up his hand to grasp hers.

Tears were in Nancy's eyes, but her sympathy with Eppie was, naturally, divided with distress on her husband's account. She dared not speak, wondering what was going on in her husband's mind.

Godfrey felt an irritation inevitable to almost all of us when we encounter an unexpected obstacle. He had been full of his own penitence and resolution to correct his error as far as the time was left to him. He was ready to do right, and he was not prepared to encounter resistance to his plan. The agitation with which he spoke again was not quite unmixed with anger.

"But I've a claim on you, Eppie—the strongest of all claims. It's my duty, Marner, to own Eppie as my child, and provide for her. She is my own child—her mother was my wife. I've a natural claim on her that must stand before every other."

Eppie had given a violent start, and turned quite pale. Silas, on the contrary, felt the spirit of resistance in him set free, not without a touch of parental fierceness. "Then, sir," he answered, with an accent of bitterness, "then, sir, why didn't you say so sixteen years ago, and claim her before I'd come to love her, i'stead o' coming to take her from me now, when you might as well take the heart out o' my body? God gave her to me because you turned your back upon her, and He looks upon her as mine. You've no right to her! When a man turns a blessing from his door, it falls to them who take it in."

"I know that, Marner. I was wrong. I've repented of my conduct in that matter," said Godfrey, who could not help feeling the edge of Silas's words.

"I'm glad to hear it, sir," said Marner, with gathering excitement. "But repentance doesn't alter what's been going on for sixteen years. Your coming now and saying 'I'm her father' doesn't alter the feelings inside us. It's me she's been calling her father ever since she could say the word."

"But I think you might look at the thing more reasonably, Marner," said Godfrey, unexpectedly awed by the weaver's direct speech. "It isn't as if she was to be taken away from you, so that you'd never see her again. She'll be very near you, and come to see you very often. She'll feel just the same toward you."

"Just the same?" said Marner, more bitterly than ever. "How'll she feel just the same for me as she does now, when we eat o' the same bit, and drink o' the same cup, and think o' the same things from one day's end to another? Just the same? That's idle talk. You'd cut us i' two."

Godfrey, not used to the weight of Marner's simple words, felt rather angry again. It seemed to him that the weaver was very selfish to oppose what was undoubtedly for Eppie's welfare. He felt himself obliged, for her sake, to assert his authority.

"I should have thought, Marner," he said, severely, "I should have thought your affection for Eppie would make you rejoice in what was for her good, even if it did call upon you to give up something. You ought to remember your own life's uncertain, and she's at an age now when her future may soon be fixed in a way very different from what it would be in her father's home. She may marry some low workingman, and then, whatever I might do for her, I couldn't make her well-off. You're putting yourself in the way of her welfare. Though I'm sorry to hurt you after what you've done, and what I've left undone, I feel now it's my duty to insist on taking care of my own daughter. I want to do my duty."

It would be difficult to say whether it were Silas or Eppie that was more deeply stirred by this last speech of Godfrey's. Eppie listened closely to the contest between her old long-loved father and this new unfamiliar father, who had suddenly come to fill the place of that black featureless shadow that had held the ring and placed it on her mother's finger. Her imagination had darted back and forth about what this revealed fatherhood implied. There were words in Godfrey's last speech that gave her some answers. Not that they determined her decision—that was determined by the feelings that vibrated in every word Silas had uttered. But they raised, even apart from these feelings, a repulsion toward the offering and the newly-revealed father.

Silas, on the other hand, was again stricken in conscience, and alarmed lest Godfrey's accusation should be true. For many moments he was mute, struggling for the composure necessary to speak. The words came out with difficulty.

"I'll say no more. Let it be as you will. Speak to the child. I'll hinder nothing."

Even Nancy, with all her sensitivity, shared her husband's view, that Marner was not justifiable in his wish to retain Eppie, after her real father had avowed himself. She felt that it was a very hard trial for the poor weaver, but her code allowed no question that a father by blood must have a claim above that of any foster father.

Besides, Nancy, used all her life to the comforts and the privileges of "respectability," could not understand the pleasures of the poor who are born poor. To her mind, Eppie, in being restored to her birthright, was reaping a too long withheld but unquestionable good. Hence she heard Silas's last words with relief, and thought, as Godfrey did, that their wish was achieved.

"Eppie, my dear," said Godfrey, looking at his daughter, not without some embarrassment, under the sense that she was old enough to judge him, "it'll always be our wish that you should show your love and gratitude to one who's been a father to you so many years, and we shall want to help you to make him comfortable in every way. But we hope you'll come to love us as well. Though I haven't been what a father should ha' been to you all these years, I wish to do the utmost in my power for you for the rest of my life, and provide for you as my only child. And you'll have the best of mothers in my wife—that'll be a blessing you haven't known in a long time."

"My dear, you'll be a treasure to me," said Nancy, in her gentle voice. "We shall want for nothing when we have our daughter."

Eppie did not come forward and curtsy, as she had done before. She held Silas's hand in hers, and grasped it firmly—it was a weaver's hand, with a palm and fingertips that were sensitive to such pressure—while she spoke with colder decision than before.

"Thank you, ma'am—thank you, sir, for your offers—they're very great, and far above my wish. For I should have no delight i' life anymore if I was forced to go away from my father, and knew he was sitting at home, thinking of me and feeling alone. We've been used to being happy together every day, and I can't think o' no happiness without him. And he says he'd nobody i' the world till I was sent to him, and he'd have nothing when I was gone. And he's took care of me and loved me from the first, and I'll stay with him as long as he lives, and nobody shall ever come between him and me."

"But you must make sure, Eppie," said Silas, in a low voice. "You must make sure that you won't ever be sorry, because you've made your choice to stay among poor folks, and with poor clothes and things, when you might ha' had everything o' the best."

His concern on this point had increased as he listened to Eppie's words of faithful affection.

"I can never be sorry, father," said Eppie. "I shouldn't know what to think on or to wish for with fine things about me, as I haven't been used to. And it 'ud be poor work for me to put on things, and ride in a gig, and sit in a place at church, as 'ud make those I'm fond of think me unfitting company for 'em. What could I care for then?"

Nancy looked at Godfrey with a pained questioning glance. But his eyes were fixed on the floor, where he was moving the end of his stick, as if he were pondering something absently. She thought there was a word that might perhaps come better from her lips than from his.

"What you say is natural, my dear child—it's natural you should cling to those who've brought you up," she said, mildly. "But there's a duty you owe to your lawful father. There's perhaps something to be given up on more sides than one. When your father opens his home to you, I think it's right you shouldn't turn your back on it."

"I can't feel that I've got any father but one," said Eppie, impetuously, while the tears gathered. "I've always thought of a little home where he'd sit i' the corner, and I should do everything for him. I can't think o' no other home. I wasn't brought up to be a lady, and I can't turn my mind to it. I like the working folks, and their food, and their ways. And," she ended passionately, while the tears fell, "I'm promised to marry a workingman, who'll live with Father, and help me to take care of him."

Godfrey looked up at Nancy with a flushed face and watering eyes. This frustration of his plan to redeem himself for the greatest error of his life made him feel the air of the room stifling.

"Let us go," he said, in an undertone.

"We won't talk of this any longer now," said Nancy, rising. "We're your well-wishers, my dear, and yours too, Marner. We shall come and see you again. It's getting late now."

In this way she covered her husband's abrupt departure, for Godfrey had gone straight to the door, unable to say more.

Chapter 20

Nancy and Godfrey walked home under the starlight in silence. When they entered the oaken parlor, Godfrey threw himself into his chair, while Nancy laid down her bonnet and shawl, and stood on the hearth near her husband, unwilling to leave him even for a few minutes, and yet fearing to say anything. At last Godfrey turned his head toward her, and their eyes met, dwelling in that meeting without any movement on either side. That quiet mutual gaze of a trusting husband and wife is like the first moment of rest or refuge from a great weariness or a great danger—not to be interfered with by speech or action.

But presently he put out his hand, and as Nancy placed hers within it, he drew her toward him, and said, "That's ended!"

She bent to kiss him, and then said, as she stood by his side, "Yes, I'm afraid we must give up the hope of having her for a daughter. It wouldn't be right to force her to come to us against her will. We can't change her bringing up and what's come of it."

"No," said Godfrey, with a keen decisiveness of tone, in contrast with his usually careless speech. "There's debts we can't pay like money debts, by paying extra for the years that have slipped by. While I've been putting off and putting off, the trees have been growing—it's too late now. Marner was in the right in what he said about a man's turning away a blessing from his door: it falls to somebody else. I wanted to pass for childless once, Nancy—I shall pass for childless now against my wish."

Nancy did not speak immediately, but after a little while she asked, "You won't make it known, then, about Eppie's being your daughter?"

"No: where would be the good to anybody?—only harm. I must do what I can for her in the state of life she chooses. I must see who it is she's thinking of marrying."

"If it won't do any good to make the thing known," said Nancy, who thought she might now allow herself the relief of entertaining a feeling which she had tried to silence before, "I should be very thankful for Father and Priscilla never to know what was done in the past, more than about Dunsey. It can't be helped, their knowing that."

"I shall put it in my will—I think I shall put it in my will. I shouldn't like to leave anything to be found out, like this of Dunsey," said Godfrey, meditatively. "But I can't see anything but difficulties that 'ud come from telling it now. I must do what I can to make her happy in her own way. I've a notion," he added, after a moment's pause, "it's Aaron Winthrop she meant she was engaged to. I remember seeing him with her and Marner going away from church."

"Well, he's very sober and industrious," said Nancy, trying to view the matter as cheerfully as possible.

Godfrey fell into thoughtfulness again. Presently he looked up at Nancy sorrowfully, and said, "She's a very pretty, nice girl, isn't she, Nancy?"

"Yes, dear, and with just your hair and eyes. I wondered it had never struck me before."

"I think she took a dislike to me at the thought of my being her father. I could see a change in her manner after that."

"She couldn't bear to think of not looking on Marner as her father," said Nancy, not wishing to confirm her husband's painful impression.

"She thinks I did wrong by her mother as well as by her. She thinks me worse than I am. But she must think it: she can never know all. It's part of my punishment, Nancy, for my daughter to dislike me. I should never have got into that trouble if I'd been true to you—if I hadn't been a fool. I'd no right to expect anything but evil could come of that marriage—and when I shirked doing a father's part too."

Nancy was silent: her spirit of rectitude would not let her try to soften the edge of what she felt to be a just remorse. He spoke again after a little while, but the tone was rather changed: there was tenderness mingled with the previous self-reproach.

"And I got you, Nancy, in spite of all. Yet I've been grumbling and uneasy because I hadn't something else—as if I deserved it."

"You've never been missing anything to me, Godfrey," said Nancy, with quiet sincerity. "My only trouble would be gone if you resigned yourself to the lot that's been given us."

"Well, perhaps it isn't too late to mend a bit there. Though it is too late to mend some things, say what they will."

Chapter 21

The next morning, when Silas and Eppie were seated at their breakfast, he said to her, "Eppie, there's a thing I've had on my mind to do, and now the money's been brought back to us, we can do it. I've been turning it over and over in the night, and I think we'll set out tomorrow, while the fine days last. We'll leave the house and everything for your godmother to take care of, and we'll make a little bundle o' things and set out."

"Where to go, Daddy?" said Eppie, in much surprise.

"To my old country—to the town where I was born—up Lantern Yard. I want to see Mr. Paston, the minister. Something may ha' come out to make 'em know I was innocent o' the robbery. And Mr. Paston was a man with a deal o' light—I want to speak to him about the drawing o' the lots. And I should like to talk to him about the religion o' this countryside, for I partly think he doesn't know of it."

Eppie was very joyful, not only about seeing a strange country, but also of coming back to tell Aaron all about it. Aaron was so much wiser than she was about most things—it would be rather pleasant to have this little advantage over him. Mrs. Winthrop, though fearful about such a long journey, was nevertheless well pleased that Silas should revisit his own country, and find out if he had been cleared from that false accusation.

"You'd be easier in your mind for the rest o' your life, Master Marner," said Dolly, "that you would. And if there's any wisdom, we've need of it i' this world, and I'd be glad of it myself, if you could bring it back."

So on the fourth day from that time, Silas and Eppie, in their Sunday clothes, with a small bundle tied in a blue linen handkerchief, were making their way through the streets of a great manufacturing town. Silas, bewildered by the changes thirty years had brought over his native place, had stopped several persons in succession to ask them the name of this town, to make sure it wasn't a mistake.

"Ask for Lantern Yard, Father—ask this gentleman with the tassels on his shoulders standing at the shop door. He isn't in a hurry like the rest," said Eppie, in some distress at her father's bewilderment, and ill at ease amidst the noise, the movement, and the multitude of strange indifferent faces.

"Eh, my child, he won't know anything about it," said Silas. "Gentlefolks didn't ever go up the Yard. But maybe somebody can tell me which is the way to Prison Street, where the jail is. I know the way out o' that as if I'd seen it yesterday."

With some difficulty, after many turns and questions, they reached Prison Street. The grim walls of the jail cheered Silas, and told him that he was in his native place.

"Ah," he said, drawing a long breath, "there's the jail, Eppie. That's just the same: I aren't afraid now. It's the third turning on the left from the jail doors—that's the way we must go."

"Oh, what a dark ugly place!" said Eppie. "How it hides the sky! It's worse than the Workhouse. I'm glad you don't live in this town now, Father. Is Lantern Yard like this street?"

"My precious child," said Silas, smiling, "it isn't a big street like this. I never was easy i' this street myself, but I was fond o' Lantern Yard. The shops here have all changed, I think—I can't make 'em out. But I shall know where to turn."

"Here it is," he said, in a tone of satisfaction, as they came to a narrow alley. "And then we must go to the left again, and then straight forward for a bit, up Shoe Lane. Then we shall be at the entry next to the o'erhanging window, where there's the nick in the road for the water to run. Eh, I can see it all."

"O Father, I feel like I'm suffocating," said Eppie. "I couldn't ha' thought any folks lived i' this way, so close together. How pretty the Stone Pits 'ull look when we get back!"

"It looks comical to me, child, now—and smells bad. I can't think it used to smell so."

Here and there a sallow, begrimed face looked out from a gloomy doorway at the strangers, and increased Eppie's uneasiness. It was a relief when they came into Shoe Lane, where there was a broader strip of sky.

"Dear heart!" said Silas. "Why, there's people coming out o' the Yard as if they'd been to chapel at this time o' day—a weekday noon!"

Suddenly he started and stood still with a look of distressed amazement that alarmed Eppie. They were before an opening in front of a large factory, from which men and women were streaming for their midday meal.

"Father," said Eppie, clasping his arm, "what's the matter?"

But she had to speak again and again before Silas could answer her.

"It's gone, child," he said, at last, in strong agitation. "Lantern Yard's gone. It must ha' been here, because here's the house with the o'erhanging window—I know that—it's just the same. But see that big factory! It's all gone—chapel and all."

"Come into that little brush shop and sit down, Father—they'll let you sit down," said Eppie, always on the watch lest one of her father's strange attacks should come on. "Perhaps the people can tell you all about it."

But neither the brush maker, who had come to Shoe Lane only ten years ago, when the factory was already built, nor any other person could tell Silas anything of the old Lantern Yard friends, or of Mr. Paston the minister.

"The old place is all swept away," Silas said to Dolly Winthrop on the night of his return. "The little graveyard and everything. The old home's gone. I've no home but this now. I shall never know whether they got at the truth o' the robbery, nor whether Mr. Paston could ha' given me any wisdom about the drawing o' the lots. It's dark to me, Mrs. Winthrop. I think it'll be dark to the last."

"Well, yes, Master Marner," said Dolly, who sat with a placid listening face, now bordered by gray hairs. "I think it may. It's the will o' Them above that many things should be dark to us. But there's some things I've never felt i' the dark about, and they're mostly what comes i' the day's work. You had hard times once, Master Marner, and it seems you'll never know the reason for it. But that doesn't hinder there being a reason, Master Marner, for all it's dark to you and me."

"No," said Silas. "No, that doesn't hinder. Since the time the child was sent to me and I've come to love her as myself, I've had light enough to trust by. Now that she says she'll never leave me, I think I shall trust till I die."

Chapter 22

There was one time of the year that was especially suitable for a wedding in Raveloe. It was when the great lilacs and laburnums in the old-fashioned gardens showed their golden and purple wealth above the mossy walls, and when there were calves still young enough to want bucketfuls of fragrant milk. People were not so busy then as they must become when the full cheese-making and the mowing season would begin. Besides, it was a time when a light bridal dress could be worn with comfort and seen to advantage.

Happily the sunshine fell more warmly than usual on the lilac tufts the morning that Eppie was married, for her dress was a very light one. She had often thought that the perfect wedding dress would be white cotton, with the tiniest pink sprig at wide intervals. When Mrs. Godfrey Cass begged to provide one, and asked Eppie to choose what it should be, she was able to give a decided answer at once.

Seen at a little distance as she walked across the churchyard and down the village, she seemed to be attired in pure white, and her hair looked like the dash of gold on a lily. One hand was on her husband's arm, and with the other she clasped the hand of her father Silas.

"You won't be giving me away, father," she had said before they went to church. "You'll only be taking Aaron as a son."

Dolly Winthrop walked behind with her husband, and that was the end of the little bridal procession. Many people were watching, and Miss Priscilla Lammeter was glad that she and her father had happened to drive up to the door of the Red House just in time to see this pretty sight. They had come to keep Nancy company today, because Mr. Cass had had to go away to Lytherley, for special reasons. That was a pity, for otherwise he might have gone, as Mr. Crackenthorp and Mr. Osgood certainly would, to look on at the wedding feast that he had ordered at the Rainbow, naturally feeling a great interest in the weaver who had been wronged by one of his own family.

"I could ha' wished Nancy had had the luck to find a child like that and bring her up," said Priscilla to her father, as they sat in the gig. "I should ha' had something young to think of then, besides the lambs and the calves."

"Yes, my dear, yes," said Mr. Lammeter. "One feels that as one gets older. Things look dim to old folks: they need have some young eyes about 'em, to let 'em know the world's the same as it used to be."

Nancy came out now to welcome her father and sister, after the wedding group had passed beyond the Red House to the humbler part of the village.

Dolly Winthrop was the first to suggest that old Mr. Macey, who had been set in his armchair outside his own door, would expect some special notice as they passed, since he was too old to be at the wedding feast.

"Mr. Macey's looking for a word from us," said Dolly. "He'll be hurt if we pass him and say nothing—and him so racked with rheumatism."

So they turned aside to shake hands with the old man. He had looked forward to the occasion, and had his prepared speech.

"Well, Master Marner," he said, in a voice that quavered a good deal, "I've lived to see my words come true. I was the first to say there was no harm in you, though your looks might be

again' you. And I was the first to say you'd get
your money back. And it's nothing but right
that you should. And I'd ha' said the 'Amens,'
and willing, at the holy matrimony. But
Tookey's done it a good while now, and I hope
you'll have none the worse luck."

In the open yard before the Rainbow the
party of guests was already assembled, though it
was still nearly an hour before the appointed
feast time. But this gave them ample time to talk
of Silas Marner's strange history, and arrive
gradually at the conclusion that he had brought
a blessing on himself by acting like a father to a
lone motherless child. Even the ferrier did not
disagree with this. On the contrary, he took it
up as peculiarly his own, and invited any hardy
person present to contradict him. But he met
with no contradiction, and the company agreed
that when a man had deserved his good luck, it
was the duty of his neighbors to wish him joy.

As the bridal group approached, a hearty
cheer was raised in the Rainbow yard. Ben
Winthrop, whose jokes had kept their acceptable flavor, decided to turn in there and receive
congratulations instead of going onto the Stone
Pits for a quiet moment with the others.

Eppie had a larger garden than she had ever
expected there now. And in other ways there
had been alterations at the expense of Mr. Cass,

the landlord, to suit Silas's larger family. He and Eppie had declared that they would rather stay at the Stone Pits than go to any new home. The garden was fenced with stones on two sides, but in front there was an open fence, through which the flowers shone, as the four united people came within sight of them.

"O Father," said Eppie, "what a pretty home ours is! I think nobody could be happier than we are."

AFTERWORD

About the Author

One of Silas Marner's greatest problems is that he feels outcast from his community, both in Lantern Yard and Raveloe. This is a feeling that the author of *Silas Marner* knew well. George Eliot suffered throughout her life from being different, in a variety of ways: her physical appearance, her intelligence, her religious beliefs, and even her romantic relationships. But though these differences caused her a great deal of anguish, eventually she would, like Silas Marner, find a place of her own in the world.

George Eliot, whose real name was Mary Ann Evans, was born in Chilvers Coton, Warwickshire, England, on November 22, 1819.

Her father was the manager of the Arbury estate, owned by a wealthy aristocrat. Evans had a happy home life, with a mother who was devoted to her children, and several siblings, including a brother, Isaac, whom she idolized. The two of them spent their time playing and running through fields around their country home.

Evans was sent away to school at age five, and would change schools often, always with her older sister. At age six she was already an avid reader, especially of Sir Walter Scott. She worked very diligently at her studies, excelling especially in languages. She could also play the piano well. At one school, a teacher named Maria Lewis took a special interest in this obviously bright child. Lewis, an Evangelical Christian, drilled Evans in elocution, and would help create the lovely musical voice that people noticed in later years. She also heavily influenced Evans in religious matters.

Evangelicalism emphasized soul-searching, and rooting out the sin in pleasure. Evans became very religious, renouncing worldly pleasure, including reading novels. She wore an unbecoming bonnet to discourage her vanity, though she was notably unattractive to begin with. She liked to lead spontaneous prayers in the classroom, and she became somewhat of an expert on the Bible. Though her fellow students admired her, she had few friends. Her personality at this stage was awkward and shy, except around her family, with whom she was more animated. However, on visits home, her extreme religiosity scared her mother a little, and Isaac teased her unmercifully.

In 1836, her mother died of cancer, and Evans left school to take charge of her father's household at the age of sixteen. She did a great deal of work in the kitchen, and oversaw the servants. This new life left her fewer opportunities to read or study, and she became very lonely and bored. But, somehow, she made time to begin a study of church history. This was the beginning of her religious doubt, when she realized that she could no longer accept her faith blindly. She also studied geometry, chemistry, and geology, and she kept studying languages, especially German. During this period, she wrote letters to Maria Lewis, discussing both the state of her soul and the job of canning jam and jelly.

When Isaac married, in 1841, he and his new wife took over managing the estate. Her father retired, and he and Evans moved to Foleshill, near Coventry. Evans was feeling very much alone, having lost her brother and the home she had grown up in. But her new neighbor secured Evans an invitation to the nearby Rosehill estate, owned by Charles and Caroline

Bray. The Brays were at the center of intellectu-
al life in Coventry, visited by Ralph Waldo
Emerson, Thomas Carlyle, and Samuel Taylor
Coleridge. Caroline's brother was Charles
Hennell, who had written a book called *An
Inquiry Concerning the Origin of Christianity*,
which Evans had already read. Along with Sara
Hennell, Caroline's sister, this group of free-
thinkers would influence Evans's thoughts on
religion and change her life dramatically.

She had already met the Brays at a social
function, but now she had her first chance to get
to know them. At Rosehill, they gave her an
enthusiastic reception, delighted by her obvious
intellectual gifts. The visit was spent discussing
philosophy, and most importantly, religion. The
Brays, though they were Christian, held beliefs
radically different from those of the traditional
Anglican church and Maria Lewis's Evangelism.
Evans felt that at last she had found people she
could talk openly with, who understood her
interests. They, in turn, liked her just as much.
They encouraged her religious skepticism, and
Evans began studying the new Biblical criticism.
As a result of her friendship with the Brays and
her new studies, she rejected her previous beliefs,
including the idea of God's vengeance and pre-
destined salvation. She was interested now main-
ly in the teachings of Jesus in the Gospels.

One Sunday, several months after moving to Foleshill, she refused to go to church with her father. To refuse to go to church because of losing faith was considered a catastrophe, as well as disrespectful toward her parent. He was so upset that he threatened to throw her out of the house. But they eventually came to a compromise: she would go to church if he would agree that she was entitled to her own beliefs.

In 1844, Evans received her first translation assignment. Charles Hennell's wife, Elizabeth Brabant, asked her to take over translating Strauss's *Das Leben Jesu* (*The Life of Jesus*) for her. This enormous task took Evans two years to complete. It was published anonymously in 1846, since it was not the kind of work that a woman would want to claim as her own. Evans spent the next two years writing for a newspaper, the Coventry *Herald*, traveling and taking care of her father, who had bouts of illness. In 1848, he became seriously ill with a weak heart, and she did little more with her hours than take care of him.

When her father died in 1849, Evans was twenty-nine. Her future was uncertain; she had no prospects for marriage, and her income was not enough to live on without working. At the insistence of the Brays, she took a continental trip with them soon after the funeral, and the travel did a lot to lift her spirits. When she came back to England, she visited her family, who were not unkind to her but made her feel that she and her radical ideas were "of no importance to any of them." So she decided to move to London. John Chapman, who had published *Das Leben Jesu*, asked her to write a book review for the *Westminster Review*, a radical publication whose prestige he wanted to revive. After approving her article, he hired her as part of the editorial staff, and she took rooms with his family in London.

John Chapman, an extremely handsome and charming man, had trained as a physician, but worked as a publisher and bookseller. He lived with both his wife and his mistress. Neither woman liked Evans's presence in the house, and they joined forces to make her life very difficult. Evans and Chapman had an ambiguous relationship, in which he confided to her about his difficulties with both women. He also took her to the theater and the opera. As she felt herself falling prey to Chapman's charms, Evans knew she should move out. When his wife caught him holding hands with Evans, the two women of the house demanded she leave, so she went back to Coventry for a while. Amazingly, however, she moved back to Chapman's after he begged her to return to the magazine.

This time, Evans was determined that their relationship would stay professional. Though her title was assistant editor, she did all of Chapman's work as the editor, letting him take all the credit. She read all the books that were reviewed, dealt with temperamental authors, and, in order to proofread articles, became knowledgeable on every subject from Ireland to atomic theory, strikes, prison reform, and "The History of the Beard." She worked herself into illness, with headaches, a cough, and rheumatism.

During this time she was involved with Herbert Spencer, an editor at the *Economist*. Their relationship did not last, and in his autobiography, Spencer insinuates that it ended because of Evans's lack of physical beauty. But Spencer would redeem himself by introducing her to his friend, a writer named George Henry Lewes. Lewes was very supportive of Evans during her demanding stint at the magazine, and eventually he became the most important person in her life.

Lewes was a scandalous choice for a woman, since he had a wife of ten years, named Agnes. Their marriage, however, was in name only, and she had had three children with different men. Lewes and his wife were separated, but they could not secure a divorce. Soon after Lewes's relationship with Evans turned romantic, Evans moved out of Chapman's and found her own lodgings. In July 1854, the couple went on a European trip, where Lewes worked on his biography of Goethe. At the end of the trip, they took rooms together in London as Mr. and Mrs. Lewes. This act shocked the community, and few people would visit them. Evans did not reveal her relationship with Lewes to her family for a few years, and when she did, her sisters wrote letters denouncing her. Her family cast her out.

In 1856, Evans began to think about writing fiction. Lewes encouraged her, and she soon began the first story of what would later be *Scenes of Clerical Life*. The story was published anonymously on New Year's Day in *Blackwood's Magazine* by Lewes's publisher, John Blackwood. *Scenes of Clerical Life* later came out under the pseudonym George Eliot. Evans chose George because it was Lewes's first name, and Eliot because she thought it was a "good mouth-filling, easily pronounced word." Evans also published *Adam Bede* as George Eliot, and the book was very successful, read and praised by Queen Victoria. It drew heavily on Evans's childhood in the country, and many readers could identify with it. No one yet knew who George Eliot was, however. Evans wrote, "There was clearly no suspicion that I was a woman . . . They thought I was the father of a family—was sure I was a man who had seen a great deal of society." One person did recognize that the work of Eliot was a woman's: Charles Dickens. He wrote her a letter, saying that if the author were not female, then "no man ever before had the art of making himself so like a woman since the world began."

When Evans's identity gradually became known in literary circles, Blackwood worried about publishing *The Mill on the Floss*, fearing the controversy over her unmarried relationship with Lewes. But he published it with Eliot's name, and it was a great success. Yet Evans was still the object of negative publicity and social ridicule, which greatly depressed her.

In 1861, she published *Silas Marner*, and then went to Italy to research her next novel, *Romola*, set in 15th-century Florence. By this time, she had earned almost 16,000 pounds, a great deal of money at that time. In 1866, she came out with *Felix Holt, the Radical*, and she also wrote collections of poetry: *The Spanish Gypsy*, *Agatha*, *The Legend of Jubal*, and *Armgart*. As Evans's fame grew, London society became more accepting of her, but her family still didn't communicate with her.

While her poetry was being published, she also began work on *Middlemarch*, widely considered her greatest work. Virginia Woolf called it "one of the few English novels written for grownup people." It was published by Blackwood from 1871-2 in parts, and it dramatically increased Evans's fame and wealth. When *Daniel Deronda* came out in 1876, Evans was generally regarded as the greatest living English novelist.

That same year, Lewes became ill with cancer, and in November, he died in London. Evans was devastated, and she refused to see anyone until February, when she agreed to meet with John Cross, her business manager and friend. She began to complete Lewes's unfinished book, *Problems of Life and Mind*.

Cross, who was twenty years younger than Evans, spent a lot of time with the author. The two became quite close, and, eventually, Cross professed his love for her. On his third proposal of marriage, she accepted. Again, Evans scandalized the community. They married in April of 1880, and went on a honeymoon to Venice. That winter, Evans became ill with kidney stones, and she died on December 22. She was buried beside George Henry Lewes in Highgate Cemetery.

Throughout the years since her death, George Eliot's work has maintained its magic for readers, mostly because of its profound insight into ordinary life and people. Yet the irony of this fact is that Eliot and her life were far from ordinary. She was a keen observer and a deep thinker who was not only honest about her beliefs, but also acted on them. These traits are rare in anyone, but doubly so in a woman of her time, something that Virginia Woolf herself acknowledged: "the burden and the complexity of womanhood were not enough; she must reach beyond the sanctuary and pluck for herself the strange bright fruits of art and knowledge."

About the Book

Silas Marner was published in 1861, and it met with success, though not as much as some of Eliot's other novels. It was written quickly—within a few months—and it was in its third edition within a year. The publisher had his doubts. He thought the novel was too somber, and needed a few "brighter lights." But Eliot maintained that, on the whole, the story was uplifting, and its popularity with readers showed she was right.

Silas Marner is still popular today, read by students in hundreds of schools. It is usually assigned because of its apparent simplicity and shortness. But a close look shows that the story is woven with many complex issues that are as relevant to readers now as they were in Eliot's time.

One of these issues is material wealth. After being cast out from Lantern Yard, Silas tries to use wealth to comfort himself. His work, once meaningful, is now merely a way to accumulate more gold. But wealth brings him no true happiness. He doesn't spend his money, because there is no one and nothing he cares about. He doesn't even care about himself enough to buy luxuries.

Material wealth is a problem even for the rich Cass family. Though they are among the wealthiest people in town, they still want more. One wonders if any amount of money would be enough to satisfy them. The desire for wealth leads Dunstan to crime, and it puts his father in an almost constant foul mood, alienating him from his sons. It also encourages Godfrey to be dishonest and heartless toward his secret wife.

Wealth and class also determine how the characters think of one another. Dunstan believes that it will be easy to talk Silas out of his money, since he does not belong to the wealthy class. When Godfrey tries to understand Silas's relationship with Eppie, he thinks that poor people must see children only as a burden on their finances. His wife, Nancy, imagines that Eppie will come to live with them, because she will naturally want a wealthier lifestyle. Eliot's wealthy characters greatly underestimate the intelligence, emotions, and values of poorer people.

Faith is another important theme of the book. Silas's first community is built around faith, and the rules of his religion cast him out from the community. Like Eliot, Silas struggles with his faith, and finally loses it. This renders him totally alone, with no higher purpose in life. He becomes a non-person, like an animal—Eliot compares him to a spider. Eventually, he learns to follow the customs of the community, for Eppie's sake. He seems to regain his faith in people, but it is not clear whether he regains his faith in God.

A surer measure of Silas's spiritual wellness might be his peculiar trances. On the one hand, they could be merely a convenient way for the author to manipulate certain events in the plot. But they could also symbolize Silas's lack of inner peace. Indeed, Mr. Macey says the trances are a sign that Silas's soul has temporarily left his body. At the end of the story, when Silas finally feels that he belongs in Raveloe, his fits seem to have subsided.

Nancy Lammeter's faith, on the other hand, remains steady, and she never questions it. She simply follows the rules she has learned from her family, church, and the Bible. But she does question herself, to see if she has lived up to these rules. Nancy's devotion to the rules makes her inflexible, and this hampers her life as well as the lives of other people. For example, she insists that she and her sister wear the same clothes, in order to show solidarity. And she refuses to adopt a child with Godfrey, because it would be defying God's plan for them. She has more faith in the rules than in people's strength or love for one another.

Nancy's faith is indeed a mixed blessing, yet there are worse cases in the novel. Eliot shows how religious faith, when taken to extremes, can turn into something hideous. In Lantern Yard, the practice of casting lots, though taken from the Bible, puts the punishment on Silas, who is innocent. In fact, it is the pious William who is guilty. He frames Silas with the crime in order to appear righteous and marry Sarah. The faith that holds the community together also tears it apart.

Certainly, the story reveals that faith is tightly connected to community, for when Silas loses one, he also loses the other. During his first fifteen years in Raveloe, he is not part of the community, and he doesn't go to church, which the townspeople find very strange. In the beginning, they make some effort to include him, because they are interested in his talent for healing and think he has magic powers. When he says he doesn't, however, they feel deceived and leave him to his isolation.

The most isolated of all the characters, though, is Molly, Godfrey's secret wife. Nobody misses her, even when she dies. Her name is hardly used by the characters or the narrator, and the reader never gets to hear her speak or interact with anyone.

Godfrey, on the other hand, is the golden boy of the town, admired by almost everyone. This makes it ironic that his fate is intertwined with two people who are so shut out from society. Yet, in a sense, Godfrey is also isolated from the community, by his wealth. He has few real friends, and no one to talk to about his problems. Despite this isolation, what Godfrey fears most is his father's and the community's disapproval—being cast out, like Silas was. He does not want to lose the only home he has, even though it is a sad one.

The idea of home also plays a large part in the story. Godfrey yearns for a better home, one with a feminine presence, bringing warmth, love, and tenderness. He feels he could be a better person if he had this home, and Nancy represents this possibility.

Marner needs a better home, as well. Though he spends nearly all his time in his house, it is time spent in misery and isolation. It is symbolic that he finds Eppie by his hearth, because she makes his house into a home. She brings love into it, and she fulfills Silas's life in a way money never could. Because he does his moral duty to her, and brings her up as his own, he finds a place in the community and a purpose for his life.

Sadly, Godfrey fails to do his duty by his first wife and Eppie, and he suffers greatly because of it. He loses the chance to be Eppie's father, and he also loses her respect. Dunstan, obviously, fails to do his duty by anyone, and gets his just desserts in the Stone Pit. William Dane deceives Silas and his community, and he simply disappears, his entire neighborhood wiped out by the building of a factory. The fates of these characters show that each person must do his or her duty openly and quickly, or worse things may happen.

And yet, as in the real world, there are some events that one cannot control with moral behavior. In other words, bad things do happen to good people, like Silas. The most damaging events in Silas's life are two thefts, and these two immoral acts by other people test his faith in God and human beings. The core of the novel is the story of his struggle, a timeless conflict that any reader can relate to. And, even better than in the real world, the struggle ends with justice being done. The worst culprits disappear or perish, while the good people, if they act morally, live happily ever after—a rule that even Nancy Lammeter would approve.